Chill

Ciara

Chill

Alex Nye

Alex Nye

Kelpies

Kelpies is an imprint of Floris Books

First published in Kelpies in 2006
Published in 2006 by Floris Books

The publisher acknowledges a Lottery grant
from the Scottish Arts Council towards the
publication of this series.

British Library CIP Data available

ISBN-10 0–86315–546–4
ISBN-13 978-086315-546-8

Produced by Polskabook, Poland

For Micah and Martha. With love.

Contents

History is a collection of found objects, washed up through time.

Jeanette Winterson

1. The Weeping Woman

Samuel was alone in the house. Outside the moor lay silent, stretching away into endless emptiness. Dunadd was completely deserted. He liked it this way, having the place entirely to himself. He could almost pretend the house was his. There was an atmosphere of secrecy and silence, which grew more intense when there was no one else about. The others had all gone skiing — it was all they could think to do on the snowbound moor. The drifts were so high that the narrow winding road, which led up to the isolated Dunadd House, had become impassable.

It was so quiet. There was nothing but the sound of the wind in the trees, and the distant murmur of the Wharry Burn, water travelling and rumbling beneath ice. The whole moor was covered with snow, an ocean of unending white, waves of it packed up against the walls of the barn and cottage — the cottage where Samuel now lived.

The rooms, corridors and staircases of Dunadd House creaked all about him in the silence. Numerous empty rooms lay behind heavy oak doors.

Samuel had felt nervous as he crossed the snowy courtyard, the white tower looming above him, but he was not going to be put off. He made his way up the silent staircase to the drawing room on the first floor.

The grandfather clock ticked noisily in the hall below, a deep sombre note befitting its age, like the heartbeat of the house itself; constant, regular, marking time.

On the wide landing dark wooden doors concealed their secrets from him, but ahead of him one door stood open. He made his way towards it over the polished boards and Turkish carpets. He trod softly, afraid to disturb the peace. The colours of the rugs were beautiful, tawny-red, crimson and tan-coloured, like the flanks and hide of a red deer. The walls were panelled in dark oak, and he was conscious that above and behind him lay another narrower stone staircase, leading into the tower, a place he had never before explored.

He passed shelves of books, old thumbed paperbacks, family favourites, and pushed open the door at the end. Before him lay the drawing room on the first floor, a vast expanse filled with light from the large bay windows on either side. Old pieces of antique furniture stood about in the shadows, gathering dust.

After a week of raging blizzards the moor had at last fallen silent, and sunlight sparkled and reflected from the snow outside, and reached into the dark corners of the house. Dust motes circulated slowly.

Samuel was familiar with this room. He had been here before, most memorably on Christmas Day, just over a week ago, although he preferred not to think about that right now. It only made him nervous, and he didn't want that. He wanted to be able to explore the house, unafraid, without feeling the need to keep glancing back over his shoulder.

He advanced slowly into the centre of the room.

Near the door stood the grand piano, as expected, its lid open and ready to play. Family photographs of the widowed Mrs Morton and her three children stood on its polished surface. At the other end of the room was a massive stone fireplace, its hearth stacked with firewood, unlit at the moment. Mr Hughes would light it later when the family returned. Above the fireplace hung the mirror, framed in elaborate scrolling gilt. Samuel made a deliberate effort not to look into it. He repeatedly drew his eyes away on purpose, especially after what he had last seen there. He didn't want that vision to disturb his dreams again.

He wanted normality, nothing unusual to happen. Or did he? Perhaps he was seeking her out again.

He walked across the drawing room to the window seat on the far side, and sat down with his back to the room. He made himself comfortable and studied the view of the mountains. It was a breathtaking panorama. The whole moor lay beneath him.

He turned his attention to the map underneath the window, a long map of the Highland line, browned with age at the edges, fixed and preserved behind glass. This is what he was here for, ostensibly, to copy the drawing of this map, so that he could have one for his own room. His bedroom in the cottage across the courtyard shared the same view. Mrs Morton had been reluctant to leave him alone in the house at first, but at last she had agreed, and now here he was.

He placed his pens and pencils on a small occasional table and dragged this into position next to him. Then he rolled out his long piece of paper, selected specially for the purpose, and pinned it down onto the table with a weight at either end to stop it from curling inwards.

The oak panelling creaked now and then in the silence, and from a long way away, if he strained his ears, Samuel could still hear the regular, soothing beat of the clock downstairs. He began to draw, his fingers moving rapidly over the paper, his back to the mirror and whatever visions it might contain.

This is an ordinary house, he told himself. *It's old and beautiful and very large, but it holds no sinister secrets.* He almost believed it for a moment.

There was nothing Samuel loved more than copying maps. He liked drawings with lots of fine lines and detail. It was a gift he'd always had. Even as a small child, sitting in front of the television, he had arranged his pens and pencils in neat rows and would draw away with utter contentment for hours.

As he worked he glanced over his shoulder from time to time at the empty room behind him. The mirror over the mantelpiece remained blank, nothing moved or stirred in its silvery depths.

He stopped drawing and listened. He thought he'd heard a sound on the staircase. The empty house waited, no sound apart from the distant tick of the grandfather clock and Samuel's own breathing. There it was again — a light tread on the stair. He decided it was probably Granny Hughes doing her dusting again, despite the fact she had been ordered to rest by Mrs Morton. She often crept about like that, duster in hand, trying to be invisible in spite of her mutterings and groanings.

He turned back to his drawing, his hand poised over the paper, and began to draw a long curving line, more slowly this time, his ear cocked for any sound outside.

Behind him the door swung slowly inwards — he could feel the draught of it at his back travelling across the room. Slowly he turned his head, but there was no one there.

Then he heard it.

It was the sound of a woman crying. It filled the room around him, permeating the walls and furniture. A bottled-up sound, trapped, as if echoing along a long dark corridor.

Samuel looked about him, spinning this way and that, but the drawing room was empty. Then he heard her footsteps. She passed through the room to the door of the library at the far end. He couldn't see her, but he could hear her footsteps clearly, and the sound of her weeping. Then the library door closed with a bang, and he was left with a terrible silence.

He dashed across the drawing room, stumbling against the furniture in his haste. When he got to the door of the library he rattled the handle furiously, but it was locked ... from the inside. He bent down and peered through the keyhole. The key was still in place. He could see nothing.

He stood up and his eye was caught by the mirror over the fireplace. It reflected back no one but himself.

"I don't believe in ghosts," he whispered to himself. "I don't believe in them." There had to be a logical explanation. *Think with the mind, not the heart.* But his mind was telling him to run.

He fled from the drawing room leaving his pens and pencils and unfinished map scattered on the window seat. The door swung wide behind him, and he pelted down the staircase, his feet clattering against the wooden boards. He charged along the corridors to the kitchen at the end, calling out for Fiona as he went.

"Fiona? Mrs Hughes?" No one answered him. Granny Hughes was up in her room in the tower, half-asleep, an unread library book on her lap.

He ran outside onto the snow-packed lawn, and stood looking up at the windows on the first floor. The immense panes of glass were dark with shadow. Nothing could be seen in the drawing room. If he closed his eyes he could still hear the sobbing echoing inside his head. He looked all about him at the silent trees, blanketed in snow, the cold bleak hills, hoping to catch a glimpse of Mr Hughes, perhaps busy about his work, or the family returning from their skiing trip, but there was no one. He stared up at the dark mass of the house. Then he thought he saw movement in the library window to the right of the drawing room. A shadow moving, backwards and forwards ... then it was gone.

"What is it, boy? What is it you've seen?"

Samuel spun round to find Mr Hughes standing behind him, a shovel in his hand where he'd been attempting to clear a path through the snow.

"I thought I heard something," Samuel stuttered, looking confused. "Something very sad."

"Oh aye?" and Mr Hughes nodded. "Uhuh! You've heard her then?" He paused and added "We heard something once, long time ago now, but it went away again right enough." It was as if they were discussing a problem of woodworm or damp, something ordinary and everyday.

Samuel stared at him. "What d'you mean?"

"Never you mind, lad. And don't go breathing a word of it to Mrs Hughes now, or she'll never do the cleaning up in that library again. And we don't want that now, do we, or Mrs Morton will get into one of her fits, so she will and start tearing her hair out ..."

Then he shuffled off through the snow without another word or backward glance.

Samuel shook his head.

He looked back at the empty windows of the big house, but this time saw nothing. The dark panes of glass simply stared back at him, empty. Whatever was inside there was watching him, he felt sure, but he didn't know why.

2. Sheriffmuir

Three weeks earlier Samuel Cunningham had moved from Edinburgh with his mother, Isabel. It was a few days before Christmas, just before the big freeze set in — not a good time to move house. The cottage on Dunadd Estate was cheap, and it was all Isabel could afford. She also knew that it would give her space for a studio workshop. She was a sculptor by profession, recycling waste in order to create imaginative works of art. She didn't earn much money from it — hardly any, in fact.

Samuel remembered the day of the move well. He placed his own belongings in a box marked "Samuel's Room," and piled it on to the back of the pick-up truck. The removal van with their heavier furniture had already left at the crack of dawn. Their flat in the tall Edinburgh tenement, now bare of furniture, looked gloomy and sad. Grey squares marked the bare walls where pictures had once hung. Samuel took one last look around.

They had never owned a car before, but travelled everywhere by bus or on foot. The white pick-up truck, which his mother had just bought a few days before, was their very first vehicle. It looked battered, but his mother insisted its engine was sound. "It's great at getting through heavy snow in winter. We'll need it up on Sheriffmuir," she'd added ominously.

The long empty hallway of the flat echoed desolately as they walked from room to room, saying a last farewell. Then they closed the door on its silence, leaving the voices to echo for another family, while they moved on and lived elsewhere.

"It's only an hour's drive away on the motorway," she kept telling him, as they drove out of Edinburgh. "You'll still be able to keep in touch with all your old friends." But that wasn't the point, and she knew it.

When they saw Stirling Castle rearing up on the skyline they knew they were nearly there. At Bridge of Allan they turned off the main road, and a winding single-track lane took them deep into some trees and up into the hills. The truck laboured its way up a steep gorge, between sheer walls of rock, where they plunged suddenly from daylight into darkness. Isabel switched on the headlights so that two cones of light shone brightly into the shadows. Then they emerged onto open moorland. At the top Samuel wound down his window to listen. Absolute silence met their ears.

He looked about him. There were only a few stark trees on the summit, bent and twisted into grotesque shapes by the wind. Samuel's fingers itched to draw them. In the distance he could see a range of mountains sweeping across the horizon, their peaks covered with snow.

As they crossed the Wharry Burn and drew nearer to Dunadd, a mist wrapped itself around the trees, obscuring the hills from view. A white five-barred gate suddenly loomed through the mist towards them.

It looked a very desolate spot.

Nailed to one of the trees was a cracked wooden sign with the one word "Dunadd" written on it. The letters were weather-worn and somehow friendly.

They drove up a steep rutted lane and at the top emerged on to a sort of high plateau, where the mist suddenly cleared. It was like being on the roof of the world. And here Samuel had his first glimpse of

Dunadd — a white chateau with a round tower, and a courtyard of outbuildings, stables, barns and cottages, one of which was to be their own. Everything was painted creamy white, including the connecting stone archways.

"Wow!" Samuel breathed, gazing about him. "It's like a monastery."

They got out of the truck and stood in the cold, empty silence.

Behind them a side door suddenly burst open and four golden retrievers came bounding out towards them, filling the air with resonant barking. They hurled themselves against the pick-up truck. Samuel's mother lost some of her bravado and flattened herself against the car, shrieking "Do something, Samuel."

They were closely followed by a small slim woman of about his mother's age, who screeched at the dogs. She looked like the sort of woman who could cope in a crisis.

"Quiet boys! Stop it at once! I said *silence!*" she bellowed in a powerful voice that echoed across the valley.

The dogs grew quiet. They stood wagging their tails and looking silly.

"I *am* sorry about that. They always greet visitors like this. They're completely harmless, you know. I'm Chris Morton, by the way," the woman said, holding out her hand to be shaken. "The door is open at the cottage, but perhaps you'd like a cup of tea first?"

"That would be lovely," Isabel smiled, trying to pull herself together. "Nice doggy," she added, aiming a pat at the smallest of the four dogs. In reply it snapped at the end of her orange scarf, and she drew back quickly.

They followed their new landlady through a side door into the big white house, through a series of dark, winding corridors until, finally, they emerged into a huge kitchen.

"Granny!" Chris Morton shrieked, her voice echoing down the passageway beyond so that Isabel jumped in alarm.

"You must meet Granny Hughes. She and her husband used to live in your cottage. They're staff on the estate, you know, but had a very hard decision to make." She lowered her voice to a conspiratorial whisper. "They were offered a council flat down in the village, an offer they couldn't possibly refuse under the circumstances. They're both pushing seventy and due for retirement, but they still come up to work in the daytime, to take care of the horses ... that kind of thing. And the children, of course!" She snorted with laughter. "I could never cope without her."

Then she put her head back and yelled "Granny!" once more. Finally a miserable-looking woman with a hacking smoker's cough and a sunken chest shuffled through the door.

"Ah, there you are, Granny," Mrs Morton smiled. "The Cunninghams have arrived."

"Oh aye?" Granny said crossly and sniffed.

"Would you be an absolute sweetie," she asked, "and make them a cup of tea?"

Granny pulled her brown cardigan across her chest and shuffled towards the kettle.

"How many children do you have?" Isabel asked hopefully.

"Three," Chris Morton said. "Two boys and a girl. Charles is the eldest, he's thirteen, then there's Sebastian, he's twelve, and Fiona, the youngest. She's eleven."

"The same age as you, Samuel," Isabel beamed.

Samuel gave an awkward grin.

"You're bound to get on," Chris Morton murmured.

"Bound to!" repeated his mother.

Granny didn't take part in any of this cosy exchange, but busied herself at the sink. Then she glanced sideways at Isabel and said, "It's a nice cottage right enough, but ... brrh!" She shook her head and muttered "You'll find it awful cauld in the winter. In the summer too, come to think of it!"

"Granny, really," and Mrs Morton gave an embarrassed laugh.

"If it's a challenge you're wanting, you'll get that right enough, living up here. The coal's heavy to carry, love," she added, glancing at Isabel's slender arms. "And awfy dirty. But no doubt you know what you're in for."

"That's Granny for you," Mrs Morton laughed a little too brightly. "Keeps us all on our toes. She and Jim will show you the ropes, especially how to work the stove."

"Huh!" Granny said gruffly, her back to the rest of them. "That stove's a mind of its own."

By now Granny's husband, Jim, had appeared, carrying a paintbrush in his hand.

"Always ask Jim if there's anything you need to know," Mrs Morton was informing them. "He keeps us all straight, don't you Jim?"

"Oh aye. Aye," Mr Hughes muttered, laughing nervously. He looked less than convinced, however.

The adults fell to talking about arrangements for the house, keys and such like, so Samuel sat down at the table and gazed about him. He had never seen a kitchen quite like this one before. There seemed to be so much wildlife for a start. A rabbit sat on a kitchen counter nibbling a lettuce, and the whole pack of dogs now seemed to be lolling under the table. There was also a cockatoo in an ornate cage, and Samuel was sure he saw a horse walk past the window.

"As I said before, we're a community here," Mrs Morton was saying. "We all pull together. Look out for one another. That sort of thing."

Isabel drew her feet under her nervously. "Of course," she murmured politely.

It was a bright and colourful room. The cabinets were all painted soft pale blue and yellow, and there were wooden dressers stacked to the ceiling with hand-painted pottery. A large red Aga heated the room nicely. There was a rocking chair and a long wooden table with bowls of fruit and candles and model aeroplanes and paintboxes scattered across it — evidence of Mrs Morton's children.

By the time Mrs Morton led them across the courtyard to view their new home, the sun had come out and burnt away the mist.

"Of course you're seeing the cottage at its best," Mrs Morton explained, as she unlocked the front door and pushed it open. "The sun doesn't always shine quite so flatteringly up here. It can be pretty bleak in the winter."

Samuel and his mother looked about them. The interior of the cottage was fairly run down, but it was large and spacious and had potential. There were fireplaces in every room, and Isabel was already having fantasies about lighting a crackling fire in each, as well as tackling that truculent stove.

She approached the mantelpiece and wiped a finger along its dusty surface, her face inscrutable. Mrs Morton watched her uncomfortably.

"It's in need of a lick of paint and some cheering up," she apologized, glancing guiltily at the bare flagged floor of the kitchen. "What you see is what you get, I'm afraid. It's so hard to know what people want in the way of original features."

Isabel turned to Chris Morton and smiled.

"It's perfect," she said.

"It would be a long-term let of course," Mrs Morton went on. "So long as we were all agreeable, I see no reason why the period of the let should not continue for as long as is convenient. I have no other plans for the cottage."

Then she left them to unpack.

It was a sturdy little cottage, long and low, with whitewashed walls and three tall chimneys, surrounded by beech trees, which partly sheltered it from the wind, for the winds were fierce up on Sheriffmuir and roared and banged about the chimneys all year long. It had a big garden, bordered by a crumbling stonewall on one side, with a white picket fence at the end, beyond which lay the hills and Dunadd Wood. On either side of it lay the outhouses, stables and barn. At the end of the garden was a small burbling stream, whose sound would become familiar to Samuel in the weeks and months ahead as he fell asleep at night.

"I think we'll be happy here, Samuel," Isabel said confidently, once they were alone. She turned to him with a look of calm certainty on her face.

They had no idea what a severe winter lay ahead.

3. Woman in the Mirror

"Reports are coming in of arctic weather conditions sweeping across Europe, expected to hit the British Isles later this week ..."

The day before Christmas Eve, it began to snow. Icy winds blew about the cottage and rattled the windows and doors.

Next door, Chris Morton looked out of the kitchen window at the big flakes falling from the sky, and sighed.

"It looks like we'd better make up a couple of beds for you in the tower room" she said grimly, turning to Granny Hughes. "Just in case. We wouldn't want to be snowed in without you."

Granny Hughes thought wistfully of her new centrally-heated flat down in the village, and wondered if there was any possibility that she and her husband could contrive to be snowed *out* rather than *in*. Timing would be the important factor, but timing always seemed to work in Mrs Morton's favour in the end, as if the powers that be knew whom to obey.

The television showed pictures of a frozen Europe, telegraph wires and electricity pylons damaged by the polar ice screeching across the continent. Then they lost reception and had to rely on the radio. Temperatures dropped to well below freezing. Chaos was sweeping the country.

In the middle of the night the blizzards worsened. When they woke on Christmas Eve, the drifts had reached the windowsills and beyond, darkening the rooms inside. Getting coal from the barn was a struggle in itself, but Samuel managed it somehow.

At one point Mrs Morton struggled through the blizzard in her thick black cape to check up on them. When they opened the door to her, there was a barrier of waist-high snow, which had been swept against the side of the cottage.

"I just came to see you're surviving," she shouted above the wind. "We're being buried alive. If you need anything, just come across."

"Would you like to come in?" Isabel asked.

"No, I'm on my way to feed the horses."

"Do you need any help?" Samuel offered heroically.

"Stay indoors," Mrs Morton warned, and then she was off with a wave, heading towards the stables.

"Well, this is different," Samuel said, peering out of the window at an almost complete white-out.

A trace of doubt had crossed Isabel's face.

"I hope I've done the right thing, bringing you here."

By Christmas morning, there was a lull in the storm. The wind stopped howling and the world lay still under a frozen white blanket, more than a metre deep. The Siberian winds had sculpted the snow into an ocean of white that covered the entire moor.

At dusk, as the trees cast purple-black shadows onto the snow, Isabel suggested they should go next door to wish the others a Merry Christmas. Samuel had met the Morton children briefly up at the boating pond, but they hadn't been particularly friendly. Charles, the eldest, was short and stocky with wild curly black hair, and had accused Samuel of trespassing on his mother's land. He had then disappeared into the thick pine trees behind the pond, without waiting for a reply.

He was simply engulfed by the darkness of the forest, never to reappear again for the rest of that afternoon. So they hadn't exactly got off to a good start, despite their mothers' assurances that they would get on like a house on fire.

His brother, Sebastian, was thin and fair with a slightly whimsical expression. He seemed laid-back, and inclined to please his brother in order to keep the peace. Fiona, the youngest, had been the friendliest of all. She had greeted him with the words "Those two idiots over there are my brothers. But don't bother about them. You get used to them after a while. I've had to." She had sounded utterly scornful.

With her icy blue eyes, and short hair as white as spun sugar he thought she looked a bit like a Viking. She had invited him to join their barbecue, cooking sausages in a small pan over an open fire, which they then ate with their fingers. He found out that their father had died several years ago, although no one seemed to want to talk about it. Mrs Morton was bringing up her three children on her own, with the help of Granny Hughes and her husband. At least they had this in common, Samuel thought. Absent fathers.

So as he crossed the courtyard in the darkness with his mother, he felt more than a little apprehensive about meeting Charles and Sebastian again.

Although the wind had dropped, the trees still roared above them. The house looked taller and more imposing at night. Its huge white tower loomed above them menacingly, and Samuel glanced up at its windows, feeling watched.

There was no answer to their knock on the outer door, apart from the barking of the dogs, so they took off their boots and coats and made their way down the long dark corridor.

Mrs Morton was in the kitchen, fetching glasses.

"Ah, you've come," she cried. "We were just about to go across and fetch you."

She handed Samuel some of the glasses to carry and they followed her past the grandfather clock in the hallway, and up a flight of spiralling stairs. The drawing room was on the first floor and a bright fire was roaring at one end.

Samuel looked about him. An impressive Christmas tree stood in one window. He'd seen its lights glittering from outside in the dark. The room was vast, with a grand piano at one end and a huge fireplace at the other. There were long bay windows on either side, overlooking the wild-looking gardens and the moor beyond.

Mrs Morton had explained to Samuel and his mother when they first moved in that Dunadd used to be a farmhouse. Bits had been added over the years, including the round tower, which made it look like a chateau. Previous owners with grandiose ideas had simply kept on building, hence its strange shape, and many passageways and corridors.

The room Samuel was now standing in was filled with dusty bookcases and stuffed animals in glass cases. Antique pictures, framed in heavy gilt, hung on the walls. There were no comfy sofas to sit on, as in Samuel's house, just ancient hard-backed chairs, stuffed with horsehair that prickled and itched when you sat down. No one was sitting anyway. They all preferred to stand.

Samuel examined the birds in the cases, their glassy eyes cold and staring.

On top of the piano were some silver-framed family photographs. There was a wedding photograph with a young Mrs Morton in bridal white, smiling at the camera, then a later photograph of her looking sad and drawn in black. There was also one of Fiona wearing a sunhat and sipping a forbidden glass of wine. Samuel gazed at the photograph.

"Had a good look?" a voice said.

He spun round. Fiona was standing right behind him.

"I'll let you off. What d'you think of the blizzard then?" She nodded her head towards the window. "Not bad, eh?"

He shrugged. "At least we'll get to miss school."

"You wish! My mother would shift the snow herself, all the way to the A9, if it means we can still go to school on time." Samuel laughed quietly. "You think I'm joking, don't you? She would! She'd hire her own snowplough or something."

"I've never known Sheriffmuir to be quite this bad," Mrs Morton was exclaiming on the far side of the room. "It snows every year, but this beats the record."

"It's minus twenty degrees, I think," Isabel murmured.

"Well, we've got our white Christmas anyway," Mrs Morton added, a little too brightly. "Poor Granny's been very depressed," she went on after a while. Samuel thought of Granny, and tried to imagine her being anything other than depressed. "She's been talking of worse to come. Insists this is the worst it's been since 1947. She's usually spot on. She's been very low, I'm afraid, very low."

"I'm sorry to hear that," Isabel murmured politely.

While the adults chatted next to the roaring blaze, Charles and Sebastian sidled off into the library, which opened off the drawing room. This seemed to make Mrs Morton nervous and edgy. Samuel glanced through the half-open door and saw a dark cavernous room, its walls lined with heavy books. It was another part of the house, which had been added about four hundred years earlier.

"Don't go in there, boys," their mother said sharply. But they took no notice. She seemed a little agitated. A cold draught swept in from the far room, and crept like a snake around their ankles. "It's so chilly in there you see, without a fire," she complained fretfully.

Samuel drew closer to the fire, and began examining the ornaments and pictures on the tall mantelpiece. Above the fireplace hung a huge elegant mirror. He caught his reflection in it, and stared at himself. There he was, in this splendid room, surrounded by all its pictures, ornaments, bookcases and stuffed animals. He glanced away for a moment, in search of Fiona, and when he looked back at the mirror he froze. Close behind him, in the reflection, stood a woman who hadn't been there before. She had black hair, coiled and drawn back from her face, and wore a long, dark-blue plaid dress. Her fierce dark eyes were fixed on his, giving him the most penetrating stare. He turned round slowly, expecting to see her standing right behind him, but there was no one there. When he looked back at the mirror, she had gone.

"What's the matter, Samuel?" his mother said, watching him. "You look a bit pale."

He turned to face the adults. Mrs Morton's eyes were on him as well.

"Er ... nothing," he murmured. Had he just seen what he thought he'd seen? His blood ran cold in his veins, like ice.

He moved away from the fire, and looked about the room, peering into every corner, starting nervously at every shadow, but there was nothing. No sign of a woman in a long dress.

I'm going mad, he thought.

Fiona was watching him. She came and stood beside him.

"Are you all right?" she whispered.

"Yes. Why shouldn't I be?" he snapped.

"No reason. I just thought you looked a bit ..."

He gave her a quick glance, but she looked away.

"They watched the Battle of Sheriffmuir from this spot you know, right where you're standing now," she said.

"Who?"

"The people who lived here three hundred years ago. My ancestors."

Samuel stared at her, this strange girl with the icy-blue eyes.

"It swept for miles," she went on. "They were slaughtered where those trees are."

Samuel gazed out at the moonlit moor and the ghostly tree branches draped in sparkling white, and tried to imagine a battle taking place below, men fighting hand to hand on the windswept hills and hollows. Would the people living here then have heard their cries, and seen them fall?

Behind him the lights suddenly flickered and went out. There were oohs and ahs from the direction of the chairs where Isabel and Mrs Morton were sitting. The whole house had been plunged into darkness.

"Don't worry," Chris Morton called in a commanding *I can cope* sort of voice. "Power cut! We've got candles."

There was a bit of scuffling and the sound of matches, followed by a small burst of light. Mrs Morton had lit a candle on the table next to her. The group gathered close to the fireplace, for comfort and reassurance as much as anything else. Firelight flickered across their faces but the rest of the room was filled with shadow. As candles were lit on the mantelpiece and danced into life, Samuel tried not to look into the mirror again, for fear of what he might see.

Then the beam of a torch appeared on the landing.

"Don't worry, Granny," Chris Morton called out. "Just a power cut. I hope this is just a temporary blip and won't last long." But she didn't sound confident. The sudden loss of electricity had a strangely calming effect on the two families, and they played a long game of monopoly on the hearthrug. Charles was accused of cheating by his brother and sister, but won the game all the same.

Towards midnight Samuel and his mother left and made their way through the dark house with the aid of a flickering candle. Shadows stretched and lengthened along the oak-panelled walls as they felt their way along. At one point Samuel heard a door closing. He turned, the hairs on the back of his neck prickling, but the passageway behind him was empty.

He had the inexplicable feeling that he was being watched.

As they opened the door onto the snowy moonlit moor a sudden breeze extinguished the candle, but they didn't need it any more so they left it on a shelf inside the boot room. Samuel felt a wave of relief on leaving the house.

Above them a figure stood at the library window, watching as they crossed the courtyard.

4. The Longest Winter

On Boxing Day, the blizzards grew worse. When Samuel woke up the cottage was freezing. He crawled from under his duvet, and pressed the light switch once, twice. Nothing happened. The power was still off.

It was Samuel's job to gather coal from the barn, so when he was dressed, he pulled on his wellies and ventured outside with the tin bucket. It was wild outside. When he reached the safety of the barn, he paused to get his breath, and listened to the wind howling and screaming past the open door.

Back inside the cottage Isabel was strutting about the kitchen wearing several jumpers but still shivering. "Where've you been with that coal?" she complained. "Let's get that stove roaring, I'm dying for a cup of tea," and both of them set to work.

So this is my new life, he thought, remembering Edinburgh wistfully. And he hadn't even set eyes on his school yet. He decided to go and see what was happening in the big house.

Despite the blizzards Isabel had already set up a studio workshop in one of the outhouses, and as Samuel pulled on his boots, she dashed across the courtyard to it, dressed in her overalls and looking dazed with creativity. Granny did not really believe in artistic pursuits of any kind, and strongly disapproved of Samuel's mother neglecting her duties in order to "knock up some silly object in her workshed."

"Call that work?" she snorted loudly as Samuel came into the kitchen. "Lot of nonsense, that's what it is."

Samuel thought it best to make no comment.

"The boys are buried away somewhere I think," Granny informed him, "but Fiona's about."

Then she produced a biscuit tin from a cupboard and slid it onto the table.

"Help yourself," she instructed him gruffly.

"Thanks," he mumbled, reaching for the tin.

"Now away you go and find her. She'll be glad of the company, I'm sure. There's a fire lit upstairs," she called after him.

Samuel made his way slowly along the dark hallway and up the spiralling staircase, trying not to think about his experiences of the night before. The house was freezing without any of the radiators working, and there was little enough natural light, it being such a dark winter's day. Upstairs in the drawing room Fiona sat close to the flames, bathed in their orange glow.

It looked a comforting sight, the huge old room filled with flickering firelight, but Samuel was still tormented by what he had seen last night. There had been something — or someone — in that mirror that he didn't wish to see again.

Fiona smiled when she saw him. "How's your mum coping without electricity?"

"Not well. She likes her creature comforts, even though it was her idea to move here in the first place."

"Parents, huh?"

"Your mum looks quite good at coping in a crisis."

"Yeah," Fiona conceded. "She's had to, I suppose, since Dad died. Running this place and everything." Samuel felt the flames hot on his face, contrasting sharply with the chill of the rest of the room.

"How old were you when he died?"

"About three. It was a long time ago. I don't remember him all that well."

There was a thoughtful silence. Samuel glanced up at the closed door of the library. Fiona followed his gaze. "We're not allowed in there. It's out of bounds."

"Why?"

"I don't know. Another one of Mum's rules."

She stared into the flames for a moment, then added "Actually, I do know why. It's because my dad died in there. It was his room, you see. He used to love working in there, reading books and painting pictures. It's filled with his stuff. Stuff we've never thrown out ... things he painted, that kind of thing. Books he liked to read. Mum's really odd about it."

Samuel gazed at the closed door. "How did he ...?"

She answered him before he could finish. "He died of shock. He saw something ... I don't know what ... and he had a weak heart. The doctors said it wouldn't have taken much to send him on his way."

"I could show you the room if you like?" she added, glancing furtively over her shoulder.

She approached the library door, and tentatively pushed it open. Cold air swept in from the closed-off room, where no fire had been lit. Samuel followed her, gazing up at the high walls lined with leather-bound books and paintings.

"What if someone catches us?" he whispered.

"It's okay," Fiona hissed.

In the centre of the room was a green leather-topped desk, where some of her father's things were carefully displayed, untouched, as if in a museum. A blotter, an old-fashioned fountain pen and bottle of ink, as well as a jar full of pens and biros. There were books everywhere. The smell of old books and soft leather filled the room.

"This is where he died," Fiona said softly, running her finger along the desk.

Samuel eyed the place apprehensively.

"You know last night," he said, "when we were all in there?" He nodded his head towards the room next door. "I saw something ... in the mirror. The figure of a woman in a long gown, with black hair. She was staring at me."

Fiona was listening to him intently, her eyes wide.

"When I turned round, there was no one there," he finished.

Instead of exclaiming with shock as he expected her to, she simply nodded her head.

"She's come back then," was all she said.

Before Samuel could respond a loud buzzing noise suddenly filled their ears, and the lights sprang on in the next room.

"Thank God," they heard a voice cry from several rooms away. "The power's back on."

The house hummed into life; lamps glowed, radiators started to tick as the vast boiler heated them up again.

"Come on," Fiona whispered. "Let's get out of here before my mum catches us."

Back in the cottage, Samuel found his mother bent over the stove, trying to get it roaring again.

"Granny Hughes was right when she said this thing has a mind of its own," she mumbled, her cheeks bright red with exertion. She was wearing a jumper that was several sizes too big for her, and there was a smear of soot across her face. "How was next door?" she asked.

"All right." He plucked an apple from the fruit bowl and began to munch it. "They're not that friendly," he admitted. "At least, Fiona is, but her brothers are a bit strange. They keep their distance."

"Try to be patient with them," Isabel advised, sitting back on her heels for a moment, poker in hand. "I don't think they're all that happy somehow."

"What d'you mean?"

She shrugged. "I don't know. I can just tell. They lost their father, remember."

"That was ages ago," Samuel said.

"Yes, but it's obviously had a profound effect on them."

Then she bent down, and began attacking the heart of the stove with the poker.

Samuel thought about the empty library full of shadows and old books, seemingly unchanged since Fiona's father had died. There was a mystery to this place, an undefined feeling of unfinished business.

Charles stood at his window, and stared blankly at the frozen world outside. His room was high up in the tower. Far below he could see the gardens and grounds mapped out beneath him, blanketed in swirling snow. He'd heard Samuel downstairs with Fiona earlier, and had thought about coming down, but had then decided not to. Why had his mother rented the cottage to the Cunninghams, when they had been perfectly all right on their own? Charles didn't like strangers. They made him nervous. He was used to having the whole of Sheriffmuir to himself, its empty hills and sparkling forests and breathtaking views. He didn't like having to share it, or admit someone else into his territory.

"Charles? Seb?" He could hear Fiona calling him from downstairs.

After a few minutes he heard her footsteps on the twisting stone staircase in the tower. She appeared in the doorway and pushed it open.

"Power's back on," she said.

"I noticed."

He was sitting at his computer now, which had hummed back into life when the electricity was restored.

"Why didn't you come down when Samuel was here?"

Charles shrugged. He didn't really know the answer himself.

"He's lonely, I think," Fiona said. "He just wants some company. He must be missing all his friends in Edinburgh."

"Not my problem," Charles said shortly.

"Charles!" she scolded. "It wouldn't hurt you to be friendly."

"It just makes me nervous, that's all. A stranger snooping about the place."

"Snooping?"

"I heard you go in the library," Charles said.

"I was only showing him round. There's nothing wrong with that. And you and Sebastian went in there last night."

"Yes, but Mum knew we were doing it."

"And that makes it all right, does it?"

"Well, at least I didn't take a stranger in there."

"Samuel's not a stranger. He's a friend."

She made as if to leave, and then paused. "He's here to stay, so you may as well get used to him."

Charles listened to her footsteps descending the narrow stone staircase. Then he turned back to the computer screen, and stared at it angrily.

"We'll see about that," he muttered to himself.

It was the dead of night. The whole house was sleeping, filled with a familiar eerie silence, punctuated only by the rhythmic ticking of the grandfather clock in the hall below.

Up in the tower, where the boys had their rooms, Charles lay on his bed, his face twitching with the thoughts and dreams that raced across his inner-eye. Pale moonlight found its way in through the narrow window and pierced the gloom.

Suddenly Charles sat up in bed and let out a cry.

He'd woken from a terrible dream; a nightmare. A woman had appeared in the room before him — not as a vague outline, but as if she were really standing there on the rug beside his bed — and had fixed him with her heavy dark eyes. "I – will – get – you," she whispered.

He blinked wildly and looked about him, wide awake now, his ashen face beaded with sweat. He shook his head, wondering if he'd only imagined it.

5. Mysterious Neighbours

Day after day blizzards roared across the country, bringing towns and cities to a halt. No one could leave Dunadd. They were completely isolated, with no prospect of escape. The moor was unrecognizable, like an Arctic wasteland. The whole of Sheriffmuir lay under a thick blanket, which all but silenced the rushing of the Wharry Burn. The Burn itself had become like glass, caught in strange fantastical shapes.

Even Mrs Morton said she had never seen anything like it, in eighteen years of living at Dunadd.

"I wonder how they're coping down at Lynns Farm?" Granny commented, staring out of the window. "MacFarlane will have enough to do, clearing the snow from his yard. And he's hardly young."

Mrs Morton gave her a strange look and left the room.

After she'd gone, Granny Hughes shook her head and sighed. "Don't say I didn't try! You would have thought she'd look out for her own neighbour."

Samuel looked up, mystified.

"Who?"

"MacFarlane, down at Lynns Farm. You'll have seen the house. Down by the waterfall?"

Samuel shook his head.

"Ach well, I suppose you cannot see it all that well 'cos of all the trees round about it. It's hidden away, right enough."

Fiona looked up from her plate. "That's another of Mum's weird rules. She doesn't like us going there."

"Had a disagreement with him once," Granny went on. "Don't know what *that* was about, but she won't hear mention of him again. Her nearest neighbour too. Her *only* neighbour in fact. I daren't suggest one of us going along to see if he's all right in all this snow."

Charles, who was sitting at the other end of the table, looked up and met Samuel's eye. "He's meant to be off his head," he informed him, with a touch of glee.

Samuel turned and stared at the frozen grounds of Dunadd beyond the kitchen window, icicles hanging like daggers from the sill. It was one more mystery to add to the many surrounding this place.

After a week of raging blizzards, the moor at last fell silent. Samuel woke up one morning and realized that the wind had stopped howling.

Big flakes of snow fell out of the sky, feathering the dry-stone walls. Samuel shovelled lumps of coal into the tin bucket, listening to the sudden stillness outside. Poking his head out of the barn door, he thought how beautiful Dunadd looked. All around him the branches of the trees had frozen solid, reaching out white fingers of glass that looked as if they would shatter in any breeze, or chime like musical bells. The world looked strangely magical. Stones and fenceposts were capped with ice. At the end of the garden stood a small fir tree, its branches bent with snow, and Samuel realized with a pang of affection that it had already become a familiar landmark of home. Whenever he looked out of their sitting room window, he could see that tree, beside the crumbling stonewall.

The coal bucket was a heavy load to drag back to the cottage, and he stopped half-way to listen to the silence.

As he stood there, an odd feeling overcame him. It was as if he were no longer alone. Surrounded by the loneliness of the moor he had the sensation that he was being watched.

He looked down at the snow at his feet. A long shadow had thrown itself in front of him, which meant that someone was standing right behind him. He spun round. As he did so, the shadow vanished. Leading away from him were footprints in the snow, as crisp and clear as if they had just been made. They led in a long line away from him, and stopped in the middle of the lawn. Then ... nothing.

All around him silent snow-covered trees stood sentinel. He peered into the darkness between the dense pine forest to his left, then across at the barn to his right. Nothing. Just him in all this emptiness.

Was someone playing a trick on him?

He shook his head, picked up the heavy bucket of coal, and made his way back to the cottage. His footsteps crunching in the snow were the only sound.

I am definitely going insane, he thought.

Charles stood in the snow, and watched Samuel disappear inside the cottage. He glanced around him, a hunted look on his face. He was nervous, edgy. He had been watching Samuel from the darkness of the trees for the past ten minutes or so, standing under the snow-laden branches, his feet frozen into blocks of ice. He'd watched Samuel emerge with the coal bucket and make his way to the barn where the coal was stored. Then he had seen him stand in the middle of the lawn and listen to the unearthly silence and stillness of the moor. But there was someone else watching as well, and Charles could feel her presence. He was haunted here in his own home where he was supposed to feel safe; haunted by threats and dire warnings that interrupted his sleep. He shook his head. It had just been a stupid dream, he told himself; it meant nothing. But as he stood there in the snow he sensed the dark-clad figure somewhere behind him, outside his line of vision. He spun round, but the figure moved and vanished, quick as lightning. It simply melted back into the darkness of the forest.

Despite the cold he felt himself beginning to sweat. Hands in pockets, he made his way back to the house. From the trees the dark figure continued to watch him. He could feel her eyes drilling into his back, but refused to look round a second time, not wanting to show that he was frightened, or that he knew she was there ... Maybe if he pretended she didn't exist, she would simply go away ...

6. Strange Noises

It was later that same day that Samuel first heard the Weeping Woman in the drawing room of Dunadd House. He had the place to himself and was attempting to copy the drawing of the map on the window seat when he was disturbed by her footsteps crossing the room. Afterwards he was badly shaken. His mother came home later that afternoon to find him outside, too afraid to go back into the house. He hadn't finished his drawing, but preferred not to do it while the house was empty and made odd sounds, he said.

"All old houses make strange noises," she told him, trying to reassure him. "Doors bang in the wind, radiators creak and wood settles. It's just what old houses do."

He said he didn't want to talk about it any more, and decided to go and wait in the kitchen for the Mortons to come home, which they did at teatime, just as it was beginning to get dark. Granny Hughes had emerged from her room, and was back at her post in the kitchen, fretting that the whole family would be lost if they stayed out much longer. Lettice the rabbit was still hopping about the worktop, which seemed to put Granny into an even worse temper.

"Be blessed if I don't cook that rabbit one day, by mistake," she muttered under her breath, wiping down the counter where the rabbit had just walked. "Wretched thing! It'll be giving us all E. Coli, so it will." Worry was fraying her nerves.

At last there came the sound of skis clattering in the boot room, and doors banging. Mrs Morton appeared, her cheeks crimson with exertion.

"Well, that was quite something," she breathed ecstatically, wrestling herself out of her padded jacket. "Didn't get as far as the village though. Bit too far."

Samuel watched them enviously, wondering what it would be like to be part of a "team" or "clan," with numbers on your side, instead of just him and his mum. He wished now he'd agreed to borrow a pair of skis and go with them, instead of staying at Dunadd to draw his stupid map.

"It was great fun," Sebastian enthused, which only made Samuel feel worse.

"Maybe next time you can come with us?" Mrs Morton suggested.

"I can't ski," Samuel reminded her.

"We can teach you. It's all a matter of confidence and trust."

"Or falling over on your backside and maybe breaking a leg," Charles added.

Mrs Morton shot him a sharp look.

He ignored her and flopped into the nearest chair. "I'm dying of hunger," he groaned.

Granny fetched them something to eat, and suddenly the kitchen was filled with the noise and bustle of the family. Samuel felt oddly comforted by it. It was hard to believe this was the same house as a few hours earlier, when he had run from the drawing room in a blind panic, to escape the sound of the Weeping Woman as she paced the upstairs rooms.

"So," Charles said, eyeing Samuel across the table as he sipped his soup. "Did he get his map finished, that's what we're all asking ourselves?"

Samuel avoided his eye.

"Charles, I wish you wouldn't speak to Samuel like that," Fiona cut in.

"Like what?"

"I didn't manage to finish it, as a matter of fact," Samuel said suddenly, glancing at the others.

Charles watched him intently.

"Why not?"

"I was disturbed." And he let the sentence hang on the air. The others looked at him expectantly, but he didn't bother to elaborate. When the boys had disappeared upstairs Fiona leant across the table towards him.

"What happened?" she asked.

"Nothing," he mumbled.

"Come on," she said. "I wasn't born yesterday."

He swallowed. "I heard her."

Fiona stared at him, wide-eyed.

"Mum said it was probably just the radiators creaking. Old houses do that, she said, make noises and things. But it wasn't that. I heard her footsteps clearly. She walked up the stairs, through the drawing room and then into the library. And all the time I could hear her sobbing."

Fiona laid her soup spoon down in the bowl. "What are we going to do?" she hissed.

"I don't know."

Upstairs in his room, in the tower, Charles switched on the computer and sat down at his desk. He felt restless. The darkness outside pressed against the window pane, and he could see nothing below. He loved having a room up here. It meant that most of the time he and Seb had complete privacy. They could hear anyone on the stone staircase long before they reached the landing. It was a bit of a nuisance now that Granny Hughes and her husband were staying in the spare room for Christmas, the room that usually remained empty. Granny didn't like staying in that room. She claimed she heard noises in the night, although nobody took much notice of her. She was always nervous, anyway. Wasn't used to big houses. Said so herself. The rest of the time he and Sebastian had the whole tower to themselves. It felt almost medieval, although it wasn't. It still had the original stone staircase, twisting round and round the thick stone walls. Charles kept thinking about what Samuel had said at the supper table, and about his dream of the other night, the woman with the dark eyes hissing the words "I – will – get – you," at him. Should he tell the others? What would be the point of that? No one would believe him anyway. He barely believed it himself. He got up and went to his brother's room.

Sebastian was stretched out on the bed, as unconcerned as ever. Nothing seemed to worry him. Charles envied him that. He leaned against the doorpost, frowning.

"What d'you think disturbed him?"

Sebastian looked up, puzzled. "Who?"

"Samuel, of course. Who d'you think?"

His brother shrugged. "I don't know. He looked a bit pale, though."

"I'd love to know what it was," Charles said.

"We could ask him?"

"Not likely. He might tell Fiona about it, though," Charles added softly, thinking out loud to himself.

"We could ask Fiona then."

Charles shook his head. "She'd never tell us."

Sebastian watched his brother in silence for a minute.

"Why does it bother you so much?"

"What?"

"Samuel, living in the cottage."

"It doesn't!"

"Yes it does. You act all the time like he's some kind of threat."

Charles didn't answer at once. He looked at his brother, and for a brief moment thought about telling him about what had been happening to him lately. But the moment didn't last long. Charles wasn't used to confiding in anyone, least of all some story about a weird woman who appeared to him in his dreams at night, hissing dark threats.

"He's snooping around," Charles said instead. "I just know he is. Why was he alone in the house in the first place?"

"He was copying the map!"

"I know that, but ... oh, never mind."

Leaving Sebastian alone, he went back to his own room to brood.

On the lawn beneath him the outside security light had clicked on, and flooded the snowy garden. Charles leant closer to the glass until his breath misted it, and peered down. Far below he could see two tiny figures, wrapped up in coats and boots, making their way under the trees. What were they talking about, he wondered? He watched until they disappeared, swallowed up by the surrounding darkness.

"Will we ever be able to get out of here, do you think?" Samuel said, kicking at the nearest snowdrift.

"It might take a while. Unless the Council can be bothered to send up a snowplough, and that doesn't seem very likely."

They stood under the trees in the dark, the white snow beneath them barred with shadows.

"Mum's pestered them on the phone every day," she went on, "but they say they have other priorities."

"So that's it," Samuel said. "We're stuck!"

"I thought you said it would be a good thing," she reminded him.

"That was before I realized this place was haunted."

"Mum wouldn't like to hear you say that. She always insists there is no ghost at Dunadd."

"Does she?"

Fiona nodded. "I heard her once at a dinner party. There was this awkward silence afterwards. None of the guests knew what to say. I remember it really well. I felt sorry for the person who said it — she gave them a right ticking off. Mum can do that, without really saying very much at all. She can make you feel *this* big." She held up her hand, and closed the gap between finger and thumb.

The pair of them were silent for a moment, thinking about the guests at the dinner party, and Fiona's mother getting cross with whoever had been foolish enough to enquire about "the ghost story." Samuel could imagine it, could picture the scene in the dining room of Dunadd House, the guests all sitting round the huge mahogany table, fire and candlelight flickering on the wooden panels behind them. Granny Hughes serving everyone with a quiet disgruntled subservience, using the best silver, which usually sat untouched on the sideboard, polished religiously every other day by Mr Hughes.

"There must be more we could find out about this Weeping Woman," Samuel insisted, glancing across at the dark mass of the house, one or two lights winking in the windows. It threw a massive shadow forward onto the snow. In the big bay window of the drawing room they could see the Christmas tree glittering in the dark.

"Maybe something in the library will tell us more," he added.

Fiona gave him a sharp look. "Not possible. Mum doesn't like us going in there without her permission. It makes her nervous. You know that."

"There must be a way," he murmured. "What about at night?"

"You realize you'll be evicted from the cottage, if Mum catches you at it?"

He shrugged his shoulders. "That's why I need your help."

She rolled her eyes. "What have I done to deserve this?"

They looked at each other in the dark as if they had just struck a bargain.

"We can be partners in crime," he whispered.

While Samuel and Fiona were making their plans, Charles was alone with his own worries. That night, after dark, he took up his torch and crept down the winding stone staircase of the tower to the first-floor landing below. He pushed open the door of the drawing room, sensing rather than seeing the shadows retreat before him. This dark house held no secrets for him, it was his home.

Or did it?

Charles crossed the drawing room and made his way to the forbidden library at the far end. He had seen and heard Fiona and Samuel snooping about in there the other day. If there were anything to find in that room then he, Charles, would be the one to find it and no one else. Samuel had no right, he fumed, no business ... It was their house, not his; it was their sorrow, their loss. Any secrets or mysteries contained within its walls were theirs to bear, a private legacy that belonged only to them, the Morton children.

He crossed the dark room to the green leather-topped writing desk in the centre. There it stood, largely untouched since the day his father died. He guessed that if there were anything worth seeing here, his mother would have confiscated it by now, secreted it away in some private hiding place, but it was worth a try. He bent down and began to search. The writing desk shuddered as he pulled open each drawer. Lots of papers burst from the drawers, old receipts and bills that had never been tidied or cleared away — his mother was not very good at throwing things out.

When he found his father's letter, written on the day he died, he sat back in the chair and stared at it for a long time. He shone the beam of the torch on it, reading the last words his father had written, then slid the letter into his pocket and carried it away with him, back to his room.

7. Dusty Secrets

Mrs Morton sat at the kitchen table, holding her mobile phone tensely to her ear. She had spent the best part of a morning trying to get through to the Council, and her nerves were in a bad state.

"I've been trying to reach you for days," she told them sharply, in her sternest possible tone.

"You and the rest of the world, madam," the man on the other end of the line replied. "Listen," he said. "We have eight major towns in the Stirlingshire area which need attending to. "You are, I believe, the only residents on Sheriffmuir?"

"Well no, as a matter of fact," she began in a tone of righteous indignation. "There is the Sheriffmuir Inn and Lynns farm as well. We all ..."

"Yes, madam, but I understand the road up on Sheriffmuir is a single track lane? With no road markings?"

"Yes, but ..."

"Then it is *not* a priority road. We may be clearing as far as the inn within the next few days, but the Council bears no responsibility for clearing the road beyond that point. And besides," the man from the Council informed her, "if we *were* to clear the snow, your children would be the only ones in an empty classroom. All the schools in the Stirlingshire area are closed until further notice."

Mrs Morton put the phone down sharply.

"I'm going back to bed," she announced to the room in general.

To help ease Mrs Morton's bad mood, Granny Hughes suggested that a bout of spring-cleaning might do the trick.

"What about getting the wee ones to clear those boxes in the attic for you? You've been meaning to do that for ages now, and never got round to it."

"Count me out," Charles said. "Too busy."

"Busy doing what?" Fiona snapped.

"Ah, can't say. Top secret."

"I'll only do it if Samuel can help me," Fiona bargained, quick as a flash.

"It's a deal," her mother agreed.

So Samuel and Fiona were assigned the task of sorting through the boxes of old toys and clothes that had been mouldering away under the eaves for the past decade.

As they climbed the narrow ladder to the attic, Samuel felt more than a little apprehensive.

"There's no light up there, by the way," Fiona told him. "The bulb went, and no one thought to replace it. So we'll have to take a torch."

They inspected the boxes and crates in the shadows, old toys spilling from them, as well as bundles of smelly moth-eaten clothes.

"Why we kept all of these things, I don't know," Fiona said. Then she rushed forward and bent down to examine an old dolls' house.

"I haven't seen that for years," she cried. "I could clean it up and put it back in my room."

"I think we're supposed to get rid of stuff, not keep it," Samuel reminded her.

Dust filled their lungs and made them cough as they sorted through the contents of the boxes. Mrs Morton had given them a supply of black bin liners, and they were to fill these with any unwanted rubbish. As they worked, Samuel noticed an old wooden chest in the corner, slightly apart from the boxes and crates they were sorting. He wondered briefly what was inside it. Its lid was firmly shut so he thought nothing more about it; they were too busy to stop and explore. Half-way through the morning the torch began to flicker on and off, as if the battery was fading. At last it went off altogether, plunging them into darkness.

"Samuel," Fiona whispered, edging nearer to him. "Are you there?"

"I'm here," he whispered back. They clung to each other in the dark. It was pitch-black, and they could see nothing in front of their faces.

"What are we going to do?" Fiona said hoarsely.

"I don't know."

"We can't move."

"Wait till our eyes have adjusted to the darkness," Samuel suggested hopefully.

But while they waited, they began to hear a sound nearby. It was the sound of breathing, gentle but definite, as if someone were in the darkness beside them. Fiona clung even tighter to Samuel's arm.

"Can – you – hear – that?" she whispered slowly.

He nodded. Then remembering she couldn't see him, he added "I hear it."

"What – is – it?"

"I don't know."

It sounded as if it was just behind him. Samuel turned his head slowly, but could see nothing. He reached out a hand, and swept the air with it, seeing if he could make contact with anything, but accidentally knocked against a crate.

"Ouch!" he hissed.

"What? What is it?"

"Nothing. I hurt my hand, that's all."

"Samuel, I don't like this."

There was a silence.

"I can't say I'm delighted by it either," came the reply.

Still the sound of gentle breathing, a thin in-drawing and releasing of breath came from the darkness behind them.

Suddenly the torch sprang back to life. Samuel grabbed it and swung its beam into the shadows behind them. There was nothing there. Absolutely nothing.

But ...

In a corner, pushed under the eaves, was the old wooden chest, which he had noticed before. Something had happened to it. Its lid had been thrust open, and the contents displayed.

Samuel stared at it.

"Is it just me, or wasn't that shut before?"

He played the torch beam over it.

Fiona nodded. "I think it was."

Both of them crept closer, and the weak torchlight picked out a pile of old linen. Fiona rummaged about, lifting old tablecloths and heavily embroidered pillow-cases.

"There's nothing here," she said.

Samuel lifted out a delicate piece of finely-stitched embroidery. "Someone was kept very busy," he commented, examining it in the half-light.

Fiona dipped her arm deeper into the chest, and suddenly felt a bundle of dry paper. She lifted the package out. It was tied with colourless ribbon that had almost completely frayed.

"What's that?" he asked, but Fiona wasn't listening. She had gone deathly quiet.

She and Samuel stared at what they'd found, examining it in the torchlight.

At first it looked like a bundle of letters, but as they turned the pages over they began to realize that these were pages torn from a journal. *"The nineteenth day of April 1708"* they read. *"My name is Catherine Morton."*

The torch began to fade again, and Fiona knocked it twice against the side of the chest in frustration.

"Damn it!" she hissed. "I want to read what it says."

"Quick. Let's take these downstairs and read them before the battery goes again."

8. Catherine's Journal

They took the bundle of papers and made their way down the rickety ladder.

Mrs Morton appeared suddenly from her room, alert to any sound.

"Finished already?" she demanded.

"Er, not quite," Fiona said. "We've binned up a few things, but we just wanted to take a break."

"I hope you haven't left it in a mess?"

"We'll get back to it in a minute," Fiona muttered, her eyes gleaming with anticipation.

"All right then," she said irritably, and turned her back on them crossly.

Charles withdrew into the shadows of the drawing room as they passed, to avoid being seen. He knew they had found something, and wanted to know what it was.

"The snow is beginning to get to her," Fiona whispered as they made their way down the staircase and along the corridor to the boot room.

Across the courtyard Samuel's cottage was empty. Isabel was buried in her studio again, hammering away at a lumpy piece of metal, a look of pure jubilation on her face. Fiona and Samuel had the privacy they needed.

They went along to Samuel's small end room, closed the door, sat on the bed and began to examine their find. The writing was faded and difficult to read, with a language and spelling that wasn't entirely familiar to them, but with careful patience they managed to decipher what it had to say. A girl spoke to them from the past, a twelve-year-old girl with a story to tell.

The nineteenth day of April 1708

My name is Catherine Morton. To mark my twelfth birthdy I have decided to begin a journal. This is it. From now on, whativer I have to say, I will say it betwixt these pages.

I have lived at Dunadd all my life, and I have a suspicion I will die heer.

My bedroom is up in the tower, above the staircase, where none other can reach me. I have two older brothers, who tease me more than they oghte. I keepe to myself.

The house is verie old. It has stoode on this muir for hundreds of years. It has been in my familly for generations, a legacy stretching far back into the past.

Needless to say, I am supposed to be educated as a lady. That is to say not educated at all, in fact, except to sit nicely and sew with a nete hand. But I'm fortunate in that we live so remote from society that I'm allowed to run free, within reason. There are the gardens, the woodes, the boating pond, and of course the muir itself, stretching away into endless emptiness like the sea lapping around an island.

Instead of sewing my sampler as I oghte, I spend my time in the hills. My brothers and I whittle bows and arrows for ourselves, and play games. Sometimes these games can become dedly earnest.

My brothers are not the most patient and mild-mannered of people, but I know how to handle them. It is their wish to bully me, but I have a manner of making them feart. They think I'm a witch because I hear voices sometimes. There are voices in the house, you see. I hear them, a boy and a girl, laughing, fighting, squeals of delight, sometimes quarrelling. Even banging. I am woken at night by their antics.

This afternoon I was in the drawing room, stitching my sampler because it was raining and we were not able to go outside to play, and I heard them again. A faint tinkle of laughter. Wicked. As if bottled-up. I looked up from my sewing and there was silence suddenly. No more voices again after that.

Mrs Fletcher was busy bustling about in the room behind me, and she tutted and said "Aye, that's right. It's good to see thee stitching thy sampler for a change, stead of gallivanting about that muir. Thou shalt have to grow accustomed to quiet pastimes now thou art growing up."

I tried not to mind at her words. I don't think I like the idea of growing up.

For my birthday I was given this booke, a leather-bound volume. Mother taught me to read and write, and she considers it will be good for me to keepe a journal.

I shall not let anyone read it, however. I am afeared they would not be plesed if they culd see what is written betwixt these pages.

Mrs Fletcher says that Mother has new-fangled ideas in teaching a wee slip of a lass to read and write, and that my father would strongly disapprove if he knew. Thankfully he is too busy to notice. So I make as if not to draw attention to myself and pretend ignorance as necesserie. Tis better this way.

Father is ... well, Father is Father.

I respect him, but I keepe my distance.

I'm learning to blend in to my surroundings. If I spend an hour a day with my head bent over my embroidry silks, then no one notices if I slip off into the woodes later with none to accompanie me.

We have a privat world up ther, beyond the boating pond. The adults see naught of how I excel at shooting and riding, or how I canst beat the boys at their own games. I can yell and holler as much as I like up ther, fire off arrows that hit the mark a thousand times.

I'm free when I'm up on the muir. As wild as my brothers. As long as Father sees naught.

The twenty-first day of April 1708

I want to write today about this new thing that has happend.

A boy from the Lynns Farm has begun to come up to Dunadd to help with the horses. He's about my age, but his mother has decided he's old enough to be employed as a stable boy, when he is not helping out on their farm.

Lynns Farm lies hidden amongst the trees in a hollow of the muir, not far from the waterfall.

As soon as I saw him I knew we could be friends. But he would not respond at first. If anything he seemed angry with me for even trying. I said I should like to help him with the grooming, but he looked at me and laughed.

"You?" he said, as if the idea amused him.

"Why not?"

He looked awkward at that.

"It's not really a task for ladies, if you see what I mean."

"Who says I am a lady?"

He laughed again, and shrugged.

Then he turned his back on me, and carried on with what he was doing. He was trying to ignore me, I culd tell. But I would not allow that.

"I can ride any horse in this stable," I told him. "Bareback," I added.

He nodded and said nothing. Unimpressd.

The boy lives with his mother and brothers on the farm as our tenants. They rent the land from my father. Perhaps that explains his awkward behaviour towards me, but I am much offended that he should put up such barriers, walls to stop us communicating.

"Why is it called the Lynns Farm?" I asked him then.

He looked at me. "It's from the Gaelic, Lin meaning waterfall? I wouldn't expect thee to know that, of course," he added.

"Shall thee come up every day?" I asked him.

He shrugged. "Can't say."

I'll look out for him, though.

It's lonely up at Dunadd. Douglas and James are not guid companie. They can turn vile if they've a mind to.

I forgot to ask the stable-boy his name.

The twenty-third day of April 1708

I found out his name today. It is Patrick. And his familie name is MacFarlane. It suits him, I think, and I told him so.

I also told him about the voices I sometimes hear. He looked at me oddly.

"Thee wants to be careful, miss," he murmured. "Thee dost not want to be taken for a witch."

I laughed. "That's what my brothers think." My eyes lit up. "It terrifies them. It's a guid way of keeping them in their place. 'I'll put a spell on you,' I tell them," and I lift my arms to demonstrate to Patrick the trick I play on them. I can put the fear of God into my brothers with that little ploy.

But Patrick did not seem amused. He carried on with his work. It does not seem as if he likes my brothers much. Who can blame him? He also can not understand why I should want to be friends with him.

"Why dost thee come here?" he asked me.

"I live here," I retorted.

"No," he said. "I mean, why here?" He motioned his hand to the stable itself.

I shrugged.

"Company!"

"Why wouldst thou seek my company?"

"Why not?"

"But we're different, thee and I," he pointed out. "Our families are different. You can read."

This seems to concern him far more than it concerns me. I turned away, hurt.

"But I have no one else," I said then. "I don't have any friends of my own age. There's just me ... and my brothers."

I made as if to leave, but he stopped me.

"Wait," he called.

I turned back.

"I suppose thee couldst help a little," he relented. "It's mucky work though, for a girl. You'll catch it if your ma sees."

"She won't," I said. "I'm very careful."

So we have become friends.

The twelfth day of May 1708

Life has brightened up since we became friends. When I've finished my sewing and bible study, and helped with the chores, I go outside to find Patrick. In the dark sweet-smelling warmth of the stable, we groom the horses together, and tell stories and talk. He listens to me as if I have something important to say. (At home

I am mostly ignored, and ridiculed by my brothers if I dare to offer an opinion).

The stable smells of hay and leather and freshly-ridden horses, and I love it. No one can see us as we talk in the shadows. And for now, no one notices what I do. I'm still too young for them to trouble with much. That will not always be the case, I know. There will come a time when things will be expected of me. Lady-like things. But I am practising the art of becoming invisible.

Sometimes, when Patrick has finished his work, we wander off onto the muir. I've shown him the boating pond at the top of Glentye, and he has shown me the waterfall near his mother's farmhouse.

These little exchanges are the currency of friendship, I told him.

"Big words," he said to me. "Those are big words thou uses. Thou 'rt becoming a proper lady."

"I'm not a lady yet," I reminded him.

The fourteenth day of June 1708

I do not want to think about what happend today. Life has been so perfect, full of interest. I am not lonely any more. I always look forward to seeing Patrick.

But today my brothers cast a shadow over that, as they do over iverething nowadays. They always have the last say. Father listens to them. It's a sad thing to say about one's own brothers, but there is an element of cruelty in them. My mother, Lady Cecilia, dotes on them and they have been raised to issue orders, to give commands, not receive them. I am afraid it has not been good for them in the end.

We were up at the boating pond, Patrick and I. We

were walking along, idling I suppose, when Douglas and James appeared from nowhere. They had been hiding in the woodes, and watching us. They towered over Patrick, crowded round him.

"What is this?" James sneered. "Our little sister with a stable-hand?"

James put his face up close to Patrick's then. "Our father doesn't pay you to idle around in his daughter's company."

"I've finished my chores for the day," Patrick responded, to which James, angry now, seized my new friend by his shirt.

"James, stop it," I cried, and pulled him off.

Patrick glared at my brother as if he wud floor him with a single blow, but he did not raise his fists.

James turned to me then. "If father gets to hear how thee has spent thy time, and what sort of company thou keeps" he hissed "thou shalt be punished as he sees fit."

He didn't need to finish his sentence. I knew how Father wud punish me.

After they'd gone and left us alone, Patrick's face seemed to close over.

"Your brother's right," he told me. "Thou shouldst be getting back."

He looked resigned, as if life was turning out only as one would expect.

"What do you mean?" I said.

"There's no sense in thee coming to the stables any more."

"But we're friends," I told him.

"No, we're not," he murmured. "You're the daughter of Sir Charles, and I'm a stable boy."

He would not look at me at first. He meant what he said. There is a stubbornness about him that I have observed before.

"Thou art my only friend," I said.

His glance flickered up at me for a moment, then he was silent. He turned away from me and began to walk down the hill, towards the white turrets of Dunadd.

He left me ther without a backward glance. I have found a friend, only to lose him again. The only real friend I have ever had. I shall visit him tomorrow in the stables, just the same.

The fifteenth day of June 1708

I have taken to locking up my journal in the ebony box in my room, just in case anyone shud decide to pry. The key I have hidden away so that no one will ever find it. The ebony box is where I kepe my treasures, things that are precious to me, although of little or no value to anyone else. I am sure that in the future my ebony box will prove useful. I shall store my most important secrets in it, and one day I shall hope to be buried with that box in my grave. Oh dear, "what a morbid thought" Mrs Fletcher wud say, "for one so young!" I am not supposed to have secrets, but already I have one or two. Enough to require a box with a key.

I went to the stables where he was working this morning, but he would not look at me. He refused to speak or meet my eye. I tried to talk to him, but I have met with a solid wall of silence. So I left again.

Up in my room at the top of the tower I have been hearing the voices of the boy and girl again. They squabble and fight, keeping me awake in the early hours, and when I look for them in the darkness, my candle picks out only shadows, the bulk of my own furniture, the bed, the table, the chest under the window. Nothing else. But I can hear them as plain as day.

Who are they? What happened to them?

I remember Patrick's words to me. "Be careful they don't take thee for a witch."

People are ignorant. Men burn witches if they've nothing better to do. In a village a few miles distant, they burnt a young girl only the other month. She'd been cursing the men in the village, they say, and when three of them died of the plague, she was held responsible.

My brothers would never accuse me. Witches are not usually from families of wealth and influence like mine, or people who are expected to spend their days sewing by candlelight. They are people with work-reddened hands, who work as Patrick works.

Here the diary entries stopped. Fiona and Samuel lifted their heads and stared at each other.

"What have we found?" he whispered.

"It's her, isn't it?" Fiona hissed. "It has to be."

A portrait of a lonely young girl had emerged, growing up isolated at Dunadd, and unable to fulfil her true potential. It was a tantalizing glimpse. The two children burned with excitement and frustration. They wanted to know more of her story, what happened to her afterwards. So many questions jostled inside their heads until they felt they would burst if they didn't find the answers. It was as if she had left behind a trail of clues for them to find; traces of herself.

"Patrick MacFarlane of Lynns Farm," Fiona breathed. "It's the same name."

"Where's the rest of the journal?" Samuel said. "There has to be more."

Fiona shook her head. "This is all there is."

Leaving the delicate papers inside Samuel's desk for sake keeping, they made their way back to the big house and resolved to finish their job up in the attic.

"It'll be a good excuse," Samuel said. "We can keep looking for the rest of the journal."

They clambered back up the narrow ladder to the mouth of the attic, and shone the torch into the darkness. Fiona nudged Samuel and pointed.

"Look at that!" she said.

"What?"

She directed the long finger of light at the trunk underneath the eaves where they'd found the journal. Long curtains of cobwebs hung down from the rafters, and they moved these aside to step closer. There was an air of total neglect about this attic. No one had been up here in years.

"Did you close the lid?" she hissed.

Samuel looked at the trunk. Its lid was now firmly shut. "I don't think so," he responded.

"Then who did?"

They moved towards the chest, and opened it. Inside, all the embroidered linen which had been spilling from its belly, and muddled up in their excitement over finding the papers, was neatly folded. So neat, so perfect, it was as if the objects inside had been carefully starched and ironed. As if the children had never touched them, never been there.

"This isn't how we left it," Fiona murmured, shining the torch into the shadows.

"No."

"Let's get out of here."

"Not till we've checked it again," Samuel insisted. He dipped his hand back into the chest.

"Samuel?" Fiona cried.

He searched frantically, but there was nothing else in there, no crackling of papers to indicate more of what they'd already found. Catherine Morton's journal was incomplete.

"This is useless," Samuel said.

"We have to go," Fiona begged him. "I'm not staying up here another minute."

Reluctantly, they left the attic behind.

"Did you manage to sort out some jumble?" Mrs Morton asked her daughter as they made their way to the kitchen.

"Sort of," she murmured. "There are a few bin bags full."

"Well, at least we've made a start. We can take it to the Charity Shop ... if we ever get out of here alive," she added gloomily.

9. Footsteps in the Library

Charles sat in his room that night, in the dark, listening to the sounds of the house. Outside the hills were silent and black. Other people wondered if they found it spooky living on Sheriffmuir. Everyone knew that a battle had been fought here in 1715 and that ghosts were said to haunt the nearby forests, but it wasn't spooky. Not really. It was their own private wilderness.

In the seclusion of his tower room, Charles took out the letter that he'd found in his father's desk, and spread it out on his pillow.

It wasn't addressed to anyone in particular, but it voiced his father's concerns and was dated the day he died.

I don't know why, but I have this feeling that something terrible is about to happen. I sit here in the familiarity of the library as I write this, a room I've always loved. There are things I find difficult to explain, to put into words. I've always been a rational sort of person, logical, exact. The truth is, this is a very old and atmospheric house; a building of one sort or another has stood on this site for centuries, so it's hardly surprising if strange whisperings from the past should persist and filter through. I've always maintained that no matter what strange occurrences should take place here in this house, there must be a scientific explanation for them. I don't hold with notions of ghosts and spirits.

However, I wish I could dismiss what I have been hearing over the years so easily. For years, since just before the children were born, I've been haunted by the sound of a weeping woman. She comes to me in my dreams, whispering dark threats. And if I'm in this room, with its long cool shadows, I hear her cross the drawing room floor towards the library, slowly pacing, wringing her hands and weeping. She has repeated this ritual for years, never leaving me in peace, taunting me. I give no credence to these nightly sounds. It's just my own imagination, I tell myself, but inside I know better. I am afraid. Mortally afraid. And I can't describe this fear to anyone, or they would think I've gone mad. Perhaps I have ...

I have these premonitions of disaster. If she appears to me in person I don't know what I will do. I don't know how I will face her; she inspires such terror in me. All I can do is hope and pray ... and wait for what I know is inevitable ...

The letter was signed Daniel Morton.

Charles read it through once, twice, then lay on his back in the moonlight, staring up at the ceiling.

Part of him longed to go next door and confide in his brother Seb, but he couldn't, because he didn't want to admit that the same thing was happening to him as had happened to his father before him. He knew what his father meant when he wrote that letter. With some deep part of himself, he *understood.*

He also knew that Fiona and Samuel were trying to find out too. By day he watched them like a hawk. He listened at doors, studied them as they walked alone in the gardens below. How much did they know, he wondered?

The following afternoon when his mother suggested they all go skiing again to lift their spirits, and Fiona backed out of it, claiming she was too tired, Charles watched his sister making her excuses.

As he set off with Sebastian and his mother through the snow, he glanced back at the house uneasily, wondering what the other two would be doing in their absence. He was half-tempted to linger, to double-back and take them by surprise. He couldn't stop thinking about it. The forest either side of him looked ghostly in the freezing light, mist caught in pockets of darkness where the branches met. He longed to turn back, but his mother wouldn't hear of it, and he was forced to go on.

He was right, of course. Fiona and Samuel had been waiting for an opportunity to explore the library when the house was empty, and now it had come. Granny and her husband were both occupied in other parts of the house, and Isabel was working in her studio. They knew they wouldn't be disturbed.

Samuel turned to Fiona once the house had fallen silent. "Right. Now's our chance."

They watched from one of the windows to make sure the others had left.

Fiona didn't feel optimistic about finding the rest of the journal. "Why would those few pages have been torn out? The rest of it must have been destroyed."

"We don't know that," Samuel said.

Fiona led the way into the dark hallway, past the grandfather clock and up the spiralling staircase. She was used to the huge old farmhouse with its turrets and tower and complicated eaves, but even she was beginning to feel a little nervous creeping around it like a couple of detectives.

In the drawing room the curtains at the big windows were drawn back.

"I love that view," Samuel murmured, taking a breath as he walked towards it.

"So do I," Fiona said. They were so high up here that often, when the valley below was filled with mist or rain, they sailed above it all, the sun breaking through. There was a feeling of elation then, as if they really were on top of the world.

"I used to have a great view in Edinburgh too. I could see the Castle from my room, all lit up at night like something out of a fairytale."

There was a pause and Fiona said, "I wonder if she loved it too."

"Who?"

"Catherine Morton."

As they stood at the window, looking at the moor, Samuel tried to make out the rooftops of Lynns Farm below.

"You can't see it from here," Fiona told him. "Too many trees."

"Your mother really worries about you going near that place, doesn't she?"

Fiona nodded. "It's another of her weird rules. We're not allowed to go there, that's all."

"Why not?"

She shrugged. "I told you, a grumpy old man lives there."

"With the same name as Patrick MacFarlane in the journal?"

"I know. Weird, isn't it? Mum doesn't get on with him for some reason."

"Why?"

"I don't know. Maybe he doesn't like our dogs wandering about. Who knows? Anyway, you heard what Charles said. He's supposed to be a bit of a weirdo."

"In what way?"

She sighed. "I don't know. No one actually says!"

They walked steadily across the polished floorboards towards the library. Fiona went first, and pushed it open.

They stepped inside, peering nervously into the shadows.

Everything was exactly as they had seen it before, dust and cobwebs hanging from the ceiling, Fiona's father's things laid out carefully on the green leather-topped desk, untouched, just as if he was about to reappear and take up his place again, doing whatever it was he was doing the day he died. It seemed to Samuel there was a heavy atmosphere in this room, some kind of tension or energy.

"Now what?" Fiona whispered.

He caught her eye. "We start looking, that's what!"

Their voices sounded loud in the silence, and they glanced nervously over their shoulders.

Fiona pulled a crimson velvet footstool towards her, and sat down. Samuel was too intrigued to sit. He touched the spine of an old book with faded gold lettering embossed on its leather cover. "She said in the diary that it was a leather-bound volume," he murmured. "We need to check every book on these shelves until we're sure it isn't here. "

They decided to take a wall each, and work through the books methodically.

"I don't trust Charles," Fiona whispered after a while, listening out for any sound in the corridor beyond. "He knows we're up to something."

"What if he comes back unexpectedly?" she added.

"We'll worry about that if it happens," Samuel said. To begin with they were quite hopeful. There were so many old volumes here, and every one that they slid from its place on the dusty shelves seemed like a distinct possibility. However, each time they inspected a book, they replaced it, disappointed. Catherine's journal was proving very elusive.

"This is going to take hours," Fiona sighed, gazing up at the ranks of books towering above her.

Samuel knew that too, but was trying not to despair. He didn't want to give in so easily. What had seemed such a good idea when they started out was turning into a mammoth task. He'd been so certain they'd find something. It was too painful to give up now.

"We'll just have to come back when we can, and keep looking," he murmured.

"How can we do that? The house is never empty like this. Not with all of us snowed in together, driving each other batty."

"We can come back at night, when everyone's asleep."

Fiona couldn't believe what she was hearing.

"You are joking, aren't you?"

But she could tell from the look on his face that he meant it. He was deadly serious.

"You're mad," she whispered. "Think of the risk!"

He shrugged and avoided her eye. "It's worth it." He bent his head and continued to search, slipping book after book from the shelf. One by one he looked at them, blowing the dust off their covers, then slid them back into place. It was clear these books hadn't been touched in years.

"Granny Hughes doesn't like dusting in here on her own when she knows the rest of the house is empty, so the library doesn't always get cleaned," Fiona pointed out. "She has a thing about the library, she won't go near it unless she has to."

"Everyone seems to have a thing about the library."

They searched on in silence. The hours passed and it didn't look as if they would ever find the rest of Catherine Morton's journal amongst the neglected books of her father's old library. They would never find out what happened to her and Patrick.

"Her diary is nearly three hundred years old, after all," Fiona said. "Why would it be sitting in the library, waiting for us to find it? It's much more likely to have been destroyed or lost."

"Then why did someone tear out the opening pages and keep them?"

"Who knows?"

As they were preparing to give up, Samuel leant against the bookcase and his gaze travelled upwards. His eye came to rest on a dark carved wooden box on top of a glass-fronted bookcase. It rang a bell for some reason, although he didn't know why. It looked very old and covered in cobwebs. "I wonder what's in there?" he murmured.

She followed his gaze. "I don't know." There were so many old things lying around the place that had been there for centuries that nothing stood out as far as Fiona was concerned. But she stopped suddenly in mid-sentence. They both heard it — a sound just outside the door, the light tread of footsteps crossing the drawing room towards them. Fiona put a finger to her lips. "Shh!" she hissed. "Listen."

They sat perfectly still, hardly daring to breathe, as the footsteps came nearer.

Suddenly Samuel let out a gasp. "She mentioned it!"

"What? Sssh? Be quiet!"

But Samuel wouldn't be silenced, in spite of whatever or whoever was waiting for them outside the door.

"She mentioned it in her journal. It's the ebony box — it's black like piano keys!" and he pointed up at the dusty old box sitting on the very top of the highest bookcase.

They stared at each other, speechless. Then the slow pacing stopped, and there was a terrible moment of suspense when Samuel and Fiona felt sure the intruder would open the door to the library and find them there. They kept very still, waiting for the door to open. At last, without warning, the footsteps began to recede.

They both let out a sigh.

"It was probably just Granny," Fiona whispered.

"It didn't sound much like her."

Samuel rose unsteadily to his feet.

"Where are you going?" Fiona cried, in a hoarse whisper.

"To see who it is."

"You can't."

But Samuel wasn't listening. "I'll be all right," he hissed, and crept towards the door. He opened it a fraction, his heart stopping. He felt sure it was just someone trying to scare them, Charles perhaps. He pushed the door gently. It swung open on its hinges with an eerie whine, and the huge drawing room lay empty before him.

There was no one else about.

He walked slowly across the length of the room towards the door at the far end, tiptoeing quietly. Just as he reached the door, it suddenly swung open in his face and he let out a short cry. There was a loud scream, and it was a moment or two before he realized that his own mother was standing before him, her face white with shock.

"Samuel, you scared the life out of me," she gasped. "What on earth are you doing creeping about like this?"

Fiona appeared behind him looking sheepish. "We were just looking for a book I'd lost."

Isabel Cunningham held a hand to her pounding heart and leant against the door-frame. "I've just been giving myself the creeps, stalking about the empty house like this. I was worried about you. Wondered where you'd got to."

"Sorry, Mum," Samuel said, and tried very hard not to snigger.

Downstairs in the kitchen Isabel put the kettle on the Aga for some tea. "I promised your mother I'd let the dogs out and keep an eye on you," she said.

"I don't need looking after. I can look after myself," Fiona retorted.

"Even so, young lady, when we've had some tea, you two can take the dogs out for some exercise."

"What are you going to do?" Samuel asked his mother.

"I've got work to do," Isabel replied shortly. And he knew that meant her sculpture. She would be busy with it all afternoon, until the cold drove her from her workshop.

As they drank their tea Samuel thought of the ebony box lying in the library, almost inaccessible. He was desperate to inspect it, but Fiona warned him that her mother and the boys would be back at any time. "We don't have time," she said. "If she catches us ..." And he knew she was right.

They retreated to Samuel's room in the cottage instead, and carefully unearthed the remains of the journal from his desk.

He scanned the fragile papers and found the paragraph he was looking for. They read it out loud.

I've taken to locking up my journal in the ebony box in my room, just in case anyone shud decide to pry. The key I have hidden away so that no one will ever find it. The ebony box is where I keepe my treasures, things that are precious to me, although of little or no value to anyone else. I am sure that in the future my ebony box will prove useful. I shall store my most important secrets in it, and one day I shall hope to be buried with that box in my grave. Oh dear, "what a morbid thought," Mrs Fletcher wud say, "for one so young!" I am not supposed to have secrets, but already I have one or two. Enough to require a box with a key.

"A box with a key!" Samuel murmured.

"Well," Fiona said, smoothing out the crackling papers, "she certainly wasn't buried with it, as she wished."

"We have to get back in the library. I want to know what's inside that box. As she says herself, boxes hold secrets sometimes. I bet we'll find the rest of the journal in there!"

"How can we?" she sighed. "When will we have another chance like this one? The others will be back soon."

But Samuel had fallen mysteriously quiet, his eyes gleaming.

"Like I said, we'll go back at night, when everyone's asleep."

"You can't do that."

"Oh yes, I can," he said.

And she knew with a horrible sinking feeling that he meant it.

10. Trouble

Charles and his brother Sebastian set off through the snow the next morning, into the woods above Dunadd. They wanted to be alone. Usually Fiona would have tagged along with them as well, but she seemed too busy these days.

"She's more interested in that boy from the cottage than us," Charles mumbled.

Sebastian cast his brother a sideways glance. "*That boy* has a name, you know. Anyway, I thought you were always glad to get rid of her? Not liking to be pestered by a kid sister, that sort of thing."

Charles said nothing.

The snow was deep and they had to work hard to make their way uphill past the boating pond, which had completely frozen over. The stones around the edge were capped with glass, and the black reeds were caught in it too. The little blue rowing-boat at the end of the jetty was trapped in the ice as if it would never break free again. Their feet scrunched on dry snow.

"I'm just trying to protect her," Charles muttered.

"Protect her?" Sebastian cried. "Well, there's a first! What from, exactly?"

"I don't know. Things have been weird lately, that's all."

Everything was white and glistening, sculpted and chiselled into strange shapes, but Charles was too preoccupied to appreciate the magic of it.

"You worry about things too much," Sebastian

pointed out. "It's all this snow. It's getting to you, being stuck on the moor like this."

If only you knew, Charles thought but didn't say a word. Sometimes the burden of his father's letter felt too heavy to carry all on his own.

Sebastian ran ahead and threw a long spear-like stick into the forest, crying "Normal life will resume shortly." Then he spun round to face his brother. "We hope."

Back at Dunadd, Isabel Cunningham stood in the middle of her workshop, and surveyed the scene before her. Scattered across the workbenches were the "instruments of her trade" as she called them, bits of wire, the bottoms of green glass bottles, multi-coloured beads and shiny pieces of material. Since moving to Sheriffmuir she had been very inspired, and felt that she had produced her best work. Her latest masterpiece was a garden ornament; a huge spider's web made from wire coathangers and old spectacle lenses. It was designed to hang in the branches of a tree, where it could catch the sunlight and sparkle like an enormous version of the real thing. It was a wintry piece to match the mood of Sheriffmuir at that moment.

She lifted her head and peered out of the small dirty pane of glass that served for a window. She still had her doubts about bringing Samuel here to live, the isolation for instance, but it was more than she could have hoped for, and Samuel had actually made friends with Fiona. They seemed to be spending an awful lot of time together. Something was really engaging them. Whatever it was, she thought it could only be a good thing. And once the snowdrifts disappeared the children would be able to go to school at last, and Samuel would make more friends. She had only to wait patiently, she decided. She lifted her coffee mug to her lips, and smiled contentedly.

Samuel went over to the window, opened the lid of his desk and took out the papers torn from Catherine Morton's journal. He looked at them closely, turning the delicate pages over in his hand. Catherine Morton was the Weeping Woman, he felt sure of it. She had written these as a child. It was a glimpse into a life shrouded in mystery.

If the evidence of her diary was anything to go by, she had been a spirited and intelligent twelve-year-old. What had happened to her in the end? What had transformed her into the Weeping Woman?

He replaced the papers in his desk, and looked up. It was snowing again. Big flakes fell out of the sky. Samuel thought that Granny Hughes must be wondering if she would ever see her centrally-heated flat again.

Samuel was still making his plans. He intended to visit the library when everyone was asleep. Pulling on his boots he went next door to find Fiona. The kitchen was empty, and when he called out her name, no one answered. Before he knew it, he was heading past the grandfather clock, and up the spiralling staircase to the drawing room on the first floor, drawn by the thought of the ebony box. He called out her name, but again no one answered.

On the threshold to the library he hesitated. It was so tempting, to step into that forbidden room, and reach the box on his own, while no one was looking. There was certainly no one about; the whole house was eerily quiet.

He took one step forward, and then someone spoke his name.

"Samuel!"

The colour drained from his face. It was Mrs Morton.

"What are you doing?"

"Looking for Fiona," he mumbled.

"You won't find her in there."

She watched him as he retreated back the way he'd come, blushing to the roots of his hair.

"She's gone out on Emperor, I think," Mrs Morton added. "Although she won't get far on a pony in this weather."

At the boating pond there was no sign of Fiona, but he could see tracks leading around the edge of it, and into the woods beyond. The forest was very dark and quiet, an enclosed world full of shadows and shifting shapes, but something drew him in. He followed the hoof prints.

He became aware of a path beneath his feet as it wound through the dense undergrowth.

Ahead of him was a narrow clearing, with a huge standing stone at the end of it. The snow had drifted up against the side of it as it stood monumental and half-forgotten.

He walked up to it, brushed the snow aside and laid a hand on its cold pitted surface.

Behind the stone he saw another path leading through the trees. There was an eerie atmosphere here and he felt nervous. After a while he suddenly burst out into the open. He stood still and gazed. Before him was a massive clearing surrounded by tall trees. In one of the treetops was an elaborate professional-looking tree house, built from timber and thatch, reached by a long ladder. The snow in the clearing was full of tracks, and a wisp of grey smoke drifted from an abandoned campfire. Samuel gazed about him, intrigued.

Suddenly something whizzed past his left ear and embedded itself in the trunk of a pine behind him. He turned and saw an arrow vibrating where it had landed. Charles and Sebastian stepped out from behind the trees.

Samuel rolled his eyes. "Might have known it was you!" Grasping the arrow, he wrenched it out from the tree and inspected its tip. "That could do some serious damage, you know!"

"It was supposed to," Charles said. "What are you doing up here?"

"Looking for Fiona." It was the second time he'd repeated that today, and so far things didn't seem to be going well.

"She's not here."

"So I see."

"Anyway, I thought she's usually hanging out with you these days," Charles pointed out. "Doesn't have time for us any more."

Samuel shrugged.

Charles eyed him suspiciously, his dark eyes unnervingly like those Samuel had seen glaring at him in the mirror on Christmas Day.

"Were you following us?" He challenged Samuel. "Because I'm warning you ..." he struggled for a moment, at a loss for words. "I'm getting fed up with all this snooping around. You and Fiona are up to something, I know it."

Samuel said nothing, but Charles hadn't finished yet.

"It's not a game, you know. Our dad died in that library. It's not some stupid detective story ..."

"I didn't say it was," Samuel stammered.

"Well, don't then," Charles snapped. "Don't snoop about. Don't lead my sister into trouble. And *don't* treat our lives like it's some kind of game for you to play. Because it isn't."

He was shouting now, and even Sebastian was looking alarmed.

"Charles, calm down!" he murmured. "It doesn't matter."

Charles spun round to face his brother, his eyes dark with fury. "You're wrong," he said. "It *does* matter."

With that Charles sped off into the trees, leaving Sebastian gaping after him.

"I'm sorry," Samuel called after him. Then he added quietly. "I'm sorry. I didn't mean to make a game out of it. I know it matters ..." But Charles wasn't waiting around to listen. He had vanished into the darkness of the forest.

Sebastian hesitated, looking uncomfortable. "I'd better go after him," he mumbled.

Samuel stood there alone in the snow, in the centre of the clearing, feeling utterly lonely. Something of what Charles had said stayed with him. Charles was deeply upset, confused and troubled by the atmosphere at Dunadd, and he was right, it wasn't a game. It was deadly serious.

He listened out for the boys, wondering if they would return, but no sound broke the silence. It didn't seem as if they would ever accept him. Sheriffmuir was their little kingdom. So far they had never had to share it with anyone else. Now Samuel and his mother had come along to change all that. It was a pity things couldn't be different, he reflected. If only Charles and Sebastian weren't so remote, and ... difficult. He wandered about the empty clearing, staring up at the tree house above.

After a moment or two a white horse and rider slowly came into focus through the darkness of the trees. It was Fiona. Emperor stepped into the clearing, and she slid off his back.

"What are you doing here?" she cried.

"Looking for you, actually. But I seem to have stumbled into trouble."

"So you've found their secret camp. They'll be furious with you, you know."

"I think Charles was furious with me for other reasons. He's upset."

"Charles is always upset."

"No, I mean he's really upset. That tree house is amazing, by the way."

"Dad had it made for the boys before he died," Fiona said, squinting up at the structure built into the treetop. "He designed it himself and they've looked after it ever since. They make repairs when it gets damaged by wind or weather." She glanced at Samuel now. "They won't be pleased you found it."

She kicked at the campfire until the wisp of smoke vanished, then turned to him. "Come on. We'd better be getting back before it gets dark. Want a lift?"

Together they headed off through the trees.

The forest was very gloomy, and they had to bend their heads low beneath the branches.

"Are you ever scared, coming through these woods on your own after dark?" Samuel asked her.

"No. Why should I be?"

They rode in silence for a few moments, two dark figures on a white horse, slowly negotiating the snowdrifts and the trees.

Samuel wondered briefly where Charles and Sebastian were, if they were still wandering about in the dark.

"Hold on tight," Fiona said, and she walked Emperor down the hill towards Dunadd at a brisk pace.

At the bottom of the hill the white tower and turrets of the house loomed up ahead, smoke pouring from the chimneys. Samuel was glad to be back.

11. The Ebony Box

That night, Samuel couldn't sleep. He got up and looked out of his bedroom window. Everything sparkled and glistened in the moonlight.

Making up his mind, he grabbed his coat and boots, opened the door and stepped outside. There was no wind tonight, and for once the huge beech trees were silent.

He crossed the courtyard and opened the side door to the big house. Mrs Morton didn't appear to worry about security, and left it unlocked day and night. He was worried the dogs would bark and wake the whole household, but thankfully they recognized him and on waking wagged their tails sleepily. He took off his boots and crept through the dark house, along its winding corridors and passageways. He stole past the sleeping cockatoo in the kitchen, who didn't so much as stir in her cage, down the hallway, past the grandfather clock, and up the spiralling staircase.

The drawing room was empty and he crept quietly across it, his feet making hardly any sound on the cold boards. Then he opened the door to the library. He had been afraid he might find it locked.

Portraits of Morton ancestors stared down on him from above, watching him with an air of disapproval. He dreaded Mrs Morton appearing in the doorway behind him. She would never forgive him this time. There would be no mistaking what he was up to, and that would be the end of it. He and his mother would be sent packing, and have to find somewhere else to live.

He looked up and saw the carved ebony box. There it was, where he had last seen it, on top of the bookcase. He breathed a sigh of relief. It was within his grasp at last. There was a sliding ladder for reaching up to the highest places, and he took this now and pushed it along the shelves, wincing at the sound it made. He climbed up, then lifted the box down in his arms, clutching it carefully like a baby so as not to drop it. It was a heavy object, and he had difficulty in getting it down the ladder. Although covered in dust and cobwebs it was beautiful and intricately carved.

He knelt on the floor with his find, and tried to open it. It was locked. He ought to have known. Her words came back at him from the past. *"The key I have hidden away so that no one will ever find it."* He sat back on his heels, gazed round the library, and let out a long sigh of defeat. It could be anywhere. Chances were it had been lost a long time ago, misplaced.

He searched the drawers of the desk, but found nothing, then he went to the little bureau under the window, and began searching its cubby-holes. He did at last locate a bundle of little keys, and tried each one for size, but none of them fitted.

He stroked the carved surface of the wooden box, wondering what use it was to him without a key. He wondered how old it was. It smelt quite ancient, an old wooden smell, time-worn and precious.

After a while he got up and went to the window. He stood looking out at the silvered garden, the little stone fountain covered in snow and draped in icicles, the archways and trellises, the stone steps set into the embankment at the end of the garden, leading the way into snow-covered woods and hills beyond.

Maybe the key would be in Catherine Morton's old room, he speculated wildly, the one that Granny

Hughes and her husband were now sleeping in. He couldn't explore there just now. Then he thought about the chest in the attic, where they'd found the papers from the journal in the first place. It was worth checking it again. If it contained her embroidery and papers from her journal, there was a distinct possibility it might also hold the key to the ebony box. It was worth a try, anyway. But dare he venture up into the attic alone, in the dark? It had been bad enough in the daytime, he thought, remembering the strange breathing sound that had started up behind them when the torch battery failed, the lid of the chest mysteriously opening and closing itself, and the objects inside folded in starched right angles as soon as he and Fiona turned their backs on it.

He took a deep breath. It had to be done.

He left the library and walked slowly through the empty drawing room, his mind set on one purpose. He made his way through the dark house to the long narrow corridor that led up into the attic. He was about to climb the rickety ladder when he realized he had no torch. It was pitch black up there. He wouldn't be able to see a thing.

He stood in the empty corridor, thinking. Then he heard a sound in a distant part of the house. Footsteps. A door closing. The flush of a toilet. He kept very still in the shadows. No one would see him if he simply didn't move. He waited for silence to fall again. Where would he find a torch? He thought about going to Fiona's room and asking for help. It was tempting. He didn't particularly relish having to climb up to the attic on his own. He crept through the silent sleeping house, down to the kitchen, and into the utility room. A huge torch sat on the counter top where he remembered seeing it. Granny used it in emergencies, when there was a power cut. Grasping this, he returned to the rickety ladder, and stealthily climbed it, step by step.

At the mouth of the attic, he shone its powerful beam into the shadows. Beyond the curtain of cobwebs hanging down from the rafters he saw the old chest where they had left it, pushed up beneath the eaves. He went towards it, trying not to think about the dark empty spaces around him, and the strange breathing sound they had heard the last time they were up here. He flung the lid of the chest open, and looked inside at all the neatly-folded pillow cases, sheets, and carefully stitched samplers, everything so fragile and threadbare that he was almost afraid to disturb them.

He began to feel around under the linen. Some were cobwebby with age, and threatened to disintegrate under his touch. Down at the bottom, under an elaborate piece of embroidery, he felt a lumpy object. A key. There was nothing to say it was the right key, however. He pulled it out, rearranged the threadbare materials as best he could, closed the lid of the chest, and made his way back to the ladder.

Before he reached the mouth of the attic, however, the torch beam failed and suddenly plunged him into darkness, just as before. He felt his breath shorten. No, this couldn't be happening to him. Not now. His scalp prickled under his hair. He stumbled towards the ladder, sliding his feet forward to make sure he didn't fall through the opening altogether. Then he clambered as quickly as he could down the narrow steps. He shook the torch in his hand, and immediately the beam sprang back to life, sending a blade of light into the shadows. He switched it off quickly, then made his way carefully back to the drawing room.

The library door stood open, and the ebony box was sitting on the floor where he had left it. He bent down and inserted the key. It fitted. It was the right key. Releasing a sigh of relief, he slowly lifted the lid of the ebony box.

It was very grimy inside, and looked as if it hadn't been opened or the contents disturbed in years. His heart beat loudly in his chest. He was now on the verge of uncovering the rest of Catherine Morton's unfinished story. Soon, all would be revealed. He peered inside, searched with his fingers. Disappointment flooded him. There was no journal inside here. Not even a few more fragments torn from the rest of the volume. There was only one thing inside the box. A small leather bag, which had partly disintegrated with age. He took the bag in his hand, and gently lifted it. Particles of broken leather fell from it, and he began to worry it would crumble away in his hands. He eased it open, and carefully put his fingers inside. He could feel a small hard object, wrapped in a piece of cloth and gently, very delicately, he brought it out into the moonlight to examine it. It was a piece of very old threadbare tartan, and when he unwrapped it there was an item of jewellery in its folds, a ring made of silver twisted into a knot with a Celtic pattern engraved on it. He looked at the contents of the bag in amazement. He hadn't found the rest of the journal, but perhaps he had found another clue to the mystery of the weeping woman and her unfinished story.

He took the silver ring between his finger and thumb and held it up to the light. Although old and tarnished, it was delicately engraved.

Then, as he felt the weight of the ring in his hand, a strange thing happened. He began to hear the sobbing again, the sad sound of weeping, echoing as if she was trapped in a long empty corridor from which there was no escape.

He listened, still holding the objects in his hand, and then, just as the sound came so close that she seemed to be inside his head, a sudden silence fell.

Samuel stared down at the ring and the tartan. How long had these things lain undisturbed in the ebony box? What was their connection with Catherine Morton? Obviously the two were linked in some way. They had to be. The ring and the tartan seemed almost to have caused her outburst of grief.

He gazed around the library. Portraits stared down at him, unforgiving, but nothing moved. No one stirred.

He wondered what he should do with the things he'd found. Should he replace them in the box and return it to the bookcase?

He began to shiver with cold. Part of him dared not move in case the Weeping Woman — or worse, Mrs Morton — was outside in the drawing room, waiting for him. He had miles and miles of dark corridors to negotiate.

Carefully, he wrapped the ring in the piece of tartan, and put them back into the disintegrating leather bag. He laid the bag back inside the ebony box; then closed the lid, and thought for a minute or two. He decided to take the box and its contents with him.

As he crossed the empty drawing room, he made a deliberate effort not to look in the mirror above the fireplace.

Out on the landing, he crept towards Fiona's room. The door was ajar, and he slipped inside. He would show her the contents of the box and the leather bag, and together they would discuss what to do about it.

Fiona's room was in darkness. The door creaked on its hinges as he pushed it open, and he paused for a minute. She was asleep in a beautiful antique four-poster bed that her mother had slept in as a girl. It was glorious, supported by great wooden posts, draped in billowing cloth, an antique in itself. Samuel could never imagine sleeping in such a bed. It would never fit into his tiny bedroom in the cottage for a start. Tentatively he moved the drapes aside.

"Fiona!" he hissed. "Wake up."

He prodded her once or twice, and she sat bolt upright.

"What the ..."

She was about to shout, but he placed a hand over her mouth.

"Shh! It's only me. Don't make any noise or you'll wake everyone."

"What are you doing?"

He looked guilty and didn't answer at first. She immediately guessed.

"I *told* you not to go in the library again, not with the family about!"

"I've got the box, Fiona," he whispered. "Look." And he lifted it up to show her. "There's no journal inside it though."

"Oh." Fiona's face fell.

"But look what else I found." And he took out the leather bag and put it in her hands. Her eyes widened in surprise. "Gently," he warned. "It's very old."

Fiona slid her hand inside the bag and pulled out the two objects. The silver ring glistened in the palm of her hand, next to the threadbare piece of tartan. She stared at them, and then looked at Samuel. "It's a love-ring," she said simply.

"How do you know?"

"Because I've seen one before."

They both gazed at the objects.

"What do you think it means?" Fiona said.

"It has something to do with her, with Catherine Morton. She says so herself in the diary, she wants to keep precious things in the box, things that mean a lot to her. And when I found these things, I heard her again. Just like before."

"Did you see her?" Fiona whispered.

Samuel shook his head.

"I wonder what happened to her in the end?" Fiona murmured, turning the silver ring over and over in her hand, so that it caught the moonlight streaming through the window.

A floorboard creaked in the corridor outside.

"Quick," Fiona hissed. "Hide."

Samuel dived under the bed, pulling the ebony box with him, and lay very still, clutching it to his chest.

Fiona pulled the covers up, pretending to be fast asleep.

A pair of feet appeared in the doorway, and hesitated for a moment. Samuel recognized those feet — they belonged to Fiona's mother. Then she turned, and walked back along the corridor.

They waited until they heard her bedroom door closing again.

"You can come out now," she hissed, her upside down head appearing over the side of the bed.

"What are we going to do with these things?"

"You take them," she said. "Keep them in the cottage. They'll be safe there."

"Safe from what?"

She shrugged. "I don't know. It just seems best somehow."

But Samuel had been thinking hard. "I think we need to do some research, about the battle that took place here. Think of the dates in the diary entries. The battle took place round about then. Maybe we can find out some more?"

They agreed to sleep on it, and tomorrow they would investigate further.

"How am I going to get out of here without being seen by your mother?" he hissed.

"You'll have to think of something. Be very quiet."

"Oh, that's helpful!"

"What d'you expect me to say? It was you who decided to break into my house in the middle of the night. Follow me," she said, getting out of bed. "But no talking!"

She led him down the spiralling staircase to the kitchen, and practically pushed him out into the cold. He stood there in his pyjamas, coat and wellies, shivering.

"See you tomorrow," she whispered, and closed the door in his face.

As Samuel crossed the courtyard back to the cottage, the box under his arm, he felt someone watching him from above. He glanced quickly up at the house. A side-window of the library overlooked this part of the drive, and as he gazed at it now, he thought he saw the shadowy outline of a figure moving across the dark pane, back and forth, back and forth. He stood still and stared, straining his eyes in the moonlight. Then it vanished.

He hoped the weeping woman would not be too disturbed by the loss of her ring.

The whole house was undisturbed by Samuel's night-time visit, and slept on, regardless. Chris Morton re-settled herself in her lonely bed, and lay on her side, gently drifting back to sleep. Granny Hughes and her husband snored in their own little guest room, dreaming about their comfortable centrally-heated flat down in the village, waiting for them to return. Fiona nodded off again surprisingly quickly after Samuel's intrusion, and Sebastian had not for one moment surfaced from unconsciousness throughout the whole night. But not everyone slept soundly.

Upstairs in his room at the top of the tower, Charles suddenly sat bolt upright in his bed, blinking. Around him the dark shadows hung, unmoving. He had had the dream again, the same dream. The dream that had haunted his father. The woman with the heavy dark eyes and almost-black hair had stood before him, at the foot of his bed, staring at him and whispering over and over in a dry, rasping, barely audible voice "I – will – get – you!"

He lay back down again, and waited for sleep to come.

12. History

A few hours later, when Samuel opened his eyes, he saw the carved ebony box sitting on his desk where he had left it the night before. He took out the brittle yellowing pages torn from the twelve-year-old Catherine Morton's journal. It was hard to believe that this was the same ebony box she had mentioned in her diary, kept here at Dunadd all those years at least since 1708. Samuel felt like a true historian or archaeologist, unearthing a story that had remained untold for three hundred years. He switched on his mother's computer in the corner of the sitting room, and it hummed into life. He was going to spend the morning doing some research.

"What's the big secret?" Fiona asked later, as they climbed the stairs to her room that afternoon. But Samuel wouldn't tell her. He merely waved a CD in front of her face, and said "This!"

His eyes were gleaming, and he looked rather pleased with himself, she could tell. "I spent the morning on the Internet," he told her. "Did a bit of research." He'd downloaded the information he was looking for, and burnt it onto CD. Now they sat together at her computer. Samuel glanced over his shoulder and murmured "Push the door to."

She did as she was told. He slid the CD into the disc drive and they waited for the screen to show his findings. Then he scrolled downwards. Fiona's eyes opened wide.

"Where did you get all this stuff?"

"Easy. I just typed *Sheriffmuir* and *battle* into Google's search engine. And this is what I came up with."

Fiona peered forward, and began to read.

On a cold and misty day in November 1715, the Highlanders gathered at a particular spot called the Gathering Stone to fight against the Government, who were trying to destroy the Highland way of life. Although Gaelic was the Highlanders' only language, they were forbidden to speak it, and it wouldn't be long before they were also forbidden to wear tartan and then forced off their lands. The Battle of Sheriffmuir on 13th November 1715 was an attempt by the Jacobites and the Highlanders to rise up against what they saw as the forces of oppression.

They came in their thousands, many men from different clans, travelling on foot from the Highlands. Their hearts were proud and their heads held high, because they felt certain that a victory would be theirs. The Government Army had horses, but horses wouldn't help them in the boggy marshland of Sheriffmuir. The Highlanders thought they'd be able to storm across on foot with their claymores and win the day, particularly as they were more in number than the enemy.

So, the night before the battle they slept in the heather and bog myrtle, wrapped in their plaids. It was a bitterly cold November night, so cold that the unexpected happened. The marsh froze over and became solid ice beneath the hooves of the Government Army. Argyll's troops were able to charge across and take them by surprise. They slaughtered the Highlanders by the hundred. Almost all of the men of one clan were wiped out in the work of one day. And the women watched from a high hill, now known as the Ladies' Knoll, and wept.

Feuds between clans were common. As the Jacobite Highlanders charged into battle, their leader shouted "This is a day we have longed for. Charge, gentlemen!" The Highlanders behind him threw off their plaids, fired their muskets, and rushed forward with their claymores. When the enemy fired back, they hesitated. But their leader cried, "Revenge! Revenge! Today for revenge, and tomorrow for mourning." And what mourning there was.

Then Samuel clicked open another file.

Lynns, or Linn in Gaelic, means "a waterfall" — from the waterfall in the nearby Wharry Burn. Lynns Farm dates from the late seventeenth century, and is said to be haunted. The low-lying, marshy ground surrounding it was frozen hard in the bitterly cold November of 1715. The heavy dragoons of the Duke of Argyll's army were thus able to charge across here against the left wing of the Jacobite army as it came pouring over the crest of the hill. The Highland army reached Lynns Farm first and the woman who lived here with her sons saw eleven Redcoat foot soldiers killed and thrown on her midden. The arrival of the Government's heavy cavalry flung the Jacobite army back over the crest of the hill with terrible slaughter, and the mounds containing the Highland dead can still be seen in front of the Gathering Stone today. Other graves can be seen on Lynns Farm.

"So the Battle of Sheriffmuir swept right through Lynns Farm," Fiona said, "where a woman lived with her sons ..."

The two of them fell silent. "Patrick MacFarlane, the young stable boy," she added. "He was probably still living there at the time. Maybe he's one of the sons mentioned."

"And your people, the Mortons, watched it from the drawing room windows," Samuel added.

"And the weeping woman?"

They looked at each other in silence.

They were thoughtful for a moment, trying to imagine the confusion and horror of the battle that had raged below Dunadd. Samuel remembered Catherine's words in her journal. *"So we have become friends. Life has brightened up now. When I've finished my sewing and bible study, and helped with the chores, I go outside to find Patrick ... He listens to me as if I have something important to say."* And then later "I have found a friend, only to lose him *again.*" Samuel began to hear in his head the cries of the wounded and dying on the field of battle, as the Highland warriors fought for their lost independence in the mist.

"The Jacobites fought against my family," Fiona announced suddenly. "Or against my ancestors at Dunadd, anyway."

"Did they?" He looked at her, perplexed.

"During the battle my family were on the side of Argyll's troops. They were Government supporters. The other farmers on the moor resented this, and never forgot it."

"Why didn't you mention this before?" Samuel said.

"I didn't think about it. It's not something we jump up and down about, to be quite honest."

"How long have the Mortons owned Dunadd?" he asked her now.

"As long as anyone can remember. And before that, it was just a kind of open barn without a roof, where drovers used to sleep on their way to market. It must have been freezing. My father's ancestors were the first to occupy it and own the land."

Fiona looked away from the computer screen and sighed. "It's all very well," she said. "But what does any of this tell us about Catherine? Nothing. She remains a complete mystery."

Samuel looked at her and grinned.

"I've got a present for you," he said.

"What?"

"I thought you might like this as a new desktop background."

He opened a further file and revealed his most exciting piece of information. There on the computer screen in front of them was an example of the tartan found in Catherine's ebony box, the small frayed square which had been carefully hidden away and preserved along with the silver ring. "The MacFarlane tartan," the text underneath it read. It was described as Jacobite. Anyone wearing it would be seen as a Jacobite warrior, prepared to fight in the cause of the Stewarts against the Hanoverian king.

Fiona stared at the screen.

"Whoever wore this tartan was no friend of your family's," Samuel murmured. "So it does tell us something about her."

"It tells us she kept a piece of Patrick's tartan, despite the fact he was a Jacobite."

Whether they had liked it or not, history had driven these two people apart. Samuel thought of the peaceful hills of Sheriffmuir, the grasses waving in the breeze, and found it difficult to imagine the place filled with the cries of the wounded and dying. So much bloodshed had taken place here, so many lives had been lost, and Scotland as a nation had made her last bid for independence. The Jacobite uprising had been suppressed until the year of Culloden in 1746, and their final defeat. The whole course of Scottish history had been influenced up on these windy heights of Sheriffmuir, a battle had been fought and lost and a woman had watched it from the windows of Dunadd and wept.

"Where is this Gathering Stone?" he asked Fiona now.

"It's hidden amongst the trees. On the far side of the road going from Dunadd. Behind the MacRae Monument."

"Can we go there?"

"Of course. It'll be heavy-going in the snow, but we can try."

They shut down the computer, and stared at the blank screen. They had more than enough to keep them guessing about what might have happened to Catherine Morton. The Weeping Woman had haunted Dunadd for years, but Samuel and Fiona felt certain they were on the verge of solving the mystery of what had happened to her. They had the journal and the objects inside the ebony box to help them. Now all they needed was to interview the old man at Lynns Farm. But first of all, Samuel wanted to see the stone where the clans had gathered the night before the battle. He wanted to imagine what it was really like, to set out across this lonely moor, knowing that a stronger enemy than yourself waited in the dips and hollows of Sheriffmuir.

13. The Gathering Stone

From an upstairs window Charles stood watching Fiona and Samuel as they made their way down the avenue of beech trees. He kept his eyes on them, until they disappeared from view.

His mother had come into the drawing room behind him and stood there in silence. She glanced over his shoulder at the two disappearing figures on the moor, then looked at Charles curiously. She knew there was something wrong with her eldest son, but she didn't know what.

"What are those two up to, I wonder?" she said, narrowing her eyes into the distance.

Charles shrugged.

Mrs Morton watched him leave the room, her face creased by a worried frown. *The sooner we can get out of here, so that the children can start school again, the better,* she thought grimly, looking out at the implacable snowdrifts that were imprisoning them on the moor. Charles' mood had been so dark lately. He was always brooding. He needed to get back into the routine of term-time.

Downstairs she came across Isabel sitting with Granny Hughes at the kitchen table, a pot of tea between them.

"How's the work going?" she asked her, helping herself to a mug from the dresser.

"Very well," Isabel mused, smiling to herself. "Couldn't be better in fact. That work shed is the perfect place for my art. It gives me room to work in, and I don't need to worry about the mess."

Granny resisted the impulse to roll her eyes, or to show too plainly what she was thinking.

"I see Fiona and Samuel are off out again?"

Isabel nodded. "Yes, they do seem to be preoccupied lately, don't they?"

"Mmm," and Mrs Morton frowned slightly as she poured tea into a mug.

"I'm worried about Charles," she confessed, looking from one to the other. Granny Hughes kept her counsel, and munched a biscuit in silence. She knew when to leave the two younger women to have their cosy tête-à-tête. *If that made them feel better, well then, let them get on with it.*

"How do you mean?" Isabel ventured nervously.

"He seems so strange lately."

Isabel listened, not knowing what to say. To be honest, she had found the Morton boys a little difficult, oddly remote and intensely private. They evidently preferred to keep themselves to themselves.

Chris Morton gazed out of the narrow window at the end of the kitchen, at the bleak white world which lay outside.

"One day this snow will melt," she sighed wistfully. "One day ..."

Isabel smiled. "It's hard to imagine it ever being anything other than winter here." It was as if she had moved to a land locked in a perpetual arctic freeze.

"Huh!" Granny said gruffly, but it was the only comment she was prepared to make. She drew her chair out from beneath her, and it scraped noisily against the tiles. "Well, some of us have work to do!"

Chris Morton's dreamy gaze didn't falter, however.

"Oh, the summers are beautiful here. You'll just have to take my word for it," she continued, ignoring

Granny's interruption. "This winter is not typical, I'm glad to say. Not typical at all ..."

"I'm glad to hear it," Isabel murmured.

As soon as Fiona and Samuel were out of sight, Charles crept out of the house away from the prying eyes of the adults. He had his own agenda.

Knowing that what he was about to do was dubious and risky in the extreme, he crunched his way through the snow to the back door of the cottage. He stood on the step, and tried the door handle. As usual, it was unlocked.

Glancing furtively over his shoulder, he pushed it open and stepped inside the dark gloomy kitchen. It was cold in here, no fires lit, no lamps on. Samuel's mother was planning on spending the best part of the day in her studio. He wiped his feet on the mat, and tiptoed across the flagged floor into the quiet sitting room beyond, and down the long hallway to Samuel's bedroom at the far end of the cottage. He felt like a burglar, creeping by stealth through someone else's house like this, but he couldn't stop now.

He located Samuel's bedroom at the far end of the cottage, the bed still unmade, the covers thrown back. The first thing that caught his eye was the wooden box on the desk under the window. It looked slightly familiar to him. Hadn't he seen it somewhere before, in their own house perhaps, in the library? At this realization, he felt less guilty about breaking into the Cunninghams' cottage. It looked as if Samuel had taken to thieving, removing objects from the house without their permission, so what did it matter if he in turn did his own share of trespassing?

He lifted the lid of the box; it creaked in the silence, and he peered nervously over his shoulder.

He looked inside, and took out the leather bag. What was this? He turned it over in his hands, took out the ring and the piece of tartan. Interesting, but they told him nothing.

As an afterthought he opened Samuel's desk and saw the bundle of brittle brown papers lying there, as if waiting to be read.

He took them out, and began to read for the first time Catherine Morton's journal. Now he too could hear her voice speaking to them from the remote past.

"The nineteenth day of April 1708. My name is Catherine Morton ..."

For several minutes he was mesmerized, his head bent over the delicate papers, absorbing their contents, listening to the unfinished story she had to tell.

He was reading the final page when he heard a sound that stopped his heart. The door of the cottage opening, and a clash of pots and pans in the sink. Isabel had come back. Closing the lid of the desk and replacing the box on it, he stealthily crept out into the hallway, his heart beating fast. What would Isabel say if she found him here?

Quickly he made his way to the front porch, halfway along the corridor — the door they never used. If it was locked, then he would be stuck, but at least he could hide in the unused porch for a while, behind the drawn curtains, until the coast was clear again. The door into the front porch squeaked as he inched it open, and he winced, wondering if she'd heard anything from the kitchen. Nothing. As luck would have it, the key of the outer-door was in the lock, so he twisted it, and stepped outside into the cold snow. The trail of footprints he left behind him would be visible to anyone passing that way, but hopefully no one would.

Fiona and Samuel walked slowly along the Sheriffmuir road, cutting a careful path over the densely-packed snow and ice. They were heading for the MacRae Monument, which loomed up ahead of them, a pyramid shape built of stone and surrounded by trees. It stood on the roadside at a particularly lonely and desolate part of Sheriffmuir. There was no traffic. The narrow roads had disappeared under the snowdrifts.

"We've got to be quick," Fiona said. "We don't want to be out here after dark."

"Wait!" Samuel stopped to read the inscription on the stone monument.

"In memory of the MacRaes killed at Sheriffmuir 13th November 1715."

According to the information from the Internet, other clans fought in the battle too, but it was the Clan MacRae who suffered the worst losses. It was their descendants who thought to erect a monument here, in their memory, two hundred years later.

They gazed at the pile of stones with the tragic inscription. "And they started the day so triumphantly too," Fiona mused.

She entered the trees and began to cut a path through the deep snow. Samuel followed her. They came at last to a clearing, and Fiona stopped. "This is where many of the men died. They were buried in great mounds."

Samuel stared through the snowy trees and the mist, and thought of the Highland warriors and Redcoat soldiers clashing here, and fighting their last. It was no wonder the place was said to be haunted by battleground ghosts.

"It all seems so peaceful now," he murmured.

They walked on in silence for a while.

Ahead of them they could just make out the soaring peak of a mountain covered in snow. It loomed through the mist, and vanished again.

They left the main path behind and struck out across the deep snowdrifts, forging a way forward until Fiona came to a standstill. They had reached a bank of trees, in front of which, rising from the snow, were the dark lines of an iron cage.

"Here it is," she said. "This is where the clans gathered the night before the battle."

As they cleared the snow from around the cage, the Gathering Stone emerged, lying flat on the ground. The cage had been added years after the battle, when vandals had broken the stone in half.

They looked down at the stone and listened to the wind sighing in the frozen branches of the trees above them, a sad sound like music.

"And what did Catherine Morton and Patrick MacFarlane have to do with it all?" Samuel asked. "Did he fight in the battle do you think, wearing his Jacobite tartan?"

One of the trees had fallen and lay on its side. Samuel rested his foot on the trunk, and gazed across the moor at the mist and cloud obscuring the distant mountain peaks.

"It's such a beautiful place, your moor."

"I know."

They were both quiet for a moment, as Samuel tried to imagine the Highlanders rallying in their thousands at this point, having tramped all the way by foot from the farthest mountains of the north.

"Seb and Charles used to come here with their swords and shields, and re-enact the battle," Fiona said. "It was one of our games."

Samuel could well imagine them dodging one another

in the mist, diving behind trees and re-appearing, or doing a Highland charge with their swords raised, their blood-curdling battle-cry ringing on the air.

"Listen, what was that?" He looked round at the ranks of frozen white trees.

"It's just the wind in the branches," Fiona assured him.

Samuel could make out a bank of solid white mist appearing in the hollow below them. It advanced towards them like an army.

"Look at that," he whispered, pointing.

"It's just the mist. Will you calm down," she hissed. "You're making me jumpy. I told you it was a bad idea to come here," she muttered.

"No, you didn't."

"Well I am now. Can you walk a bit faster? We'd better be heading back before it gets dark." Their feet were frozen, despite their boots and thick socks.

"What about Lynns farm?" Samuel asked.

Fiona looked at him in disbelief. "It's a bit late for that now. We'll have to leave it till tomorrow. We don't want to get caught out in this," she added as snowflakes began to spiral out of a darkening sky. It clung to everything, their gloves and scarves, muffling the hills in more silence.

"You're right," he agreed.

They began to make their way back to the road.

"Have you ever met Mr MacFarlane before?" Samuel asked.

She shook her head. "He's a bit of a recluse. Mum's met him though. They didn't exactly see eye to eye."

At last they burst out from under the trees onto the road again, the monument in front of them.

As they began to trudge uphill towards Dunadd, Fiona stopped and pointed.

"Look. See that?" Below them, in the dip of the land, surrounded by a thick band of snow-covered trees, lay the rooftop and chimneys of a little white farmhouse which Samuel had never seen before. "Lynns Farm," she announced.

It looked a dark and gloomy place, slightly sinister with an air of neglect about it. Samuel wasn't sure he liked the idea of having to go there. Mr MacFarlane did not sound like the sort of man who encouraged visitors.

By the time they reached Dunadd it was dark and the adults had begun to worry. As they walked into the kitchen of the big house, a great fuss broke out. Fiona and Samuel were given a good talking to by not one, but three anxious females — Mrs Morton, Granny Hughes and Isabel Cunningham. All three women had a great deal to say on the subject.

As Samuel and his mother made to leave, Fiona stopped him in the corridor and they began to whisper about their plans for the next day.

"Are you still on for tomorrow?" she hissed. "Lynns Farm?"

He nodded.

"We won't go together though," she whispered, "in case my Mum starts getting suspicious. Meet me at the waterfall at nine o' clock tomorrow morning."

As she finished speaking Samuel thought he heard a door quietly closing behind them. He turned his head, but the corridor was empty.

"Really, Samuel, I don't know what you and Fiona could have been thinking about, wandering about the moor after dark. It could be very dangerous, you know," Isabel berated him, as they made their way across the courtyard back to the cottage.

"I know, Mum, I'm sorry," he said. "It only started to get dark when we were nearly home."

"That's not the point. Don't let it happen again. I've aged about ten years this afternoon. I hadn't even realized you were missing until Granny Hughes started fretting about it."

Samuel decided the best policy was to apologize as often as possible. They opened the door of the cottage, only to find the stove had gone out again.

"Blast," Isabel muttered, as she set to work to rescue it. Samuel made his way to his own room.

There, on his desk under the window, was the carved ebony box in which had been stored secret treasures from the past. In unlocking the box, they had unlocked more of that mysterious past. Now Samuel picked up the fragments torn from Catherine Morton's journal, and placed them beside the leather bag, containing the ring and the piece of tartan. These objects belonged together, he decided. Inside the ebony box, where she would have wanted them.

As he glanced about the room he noticed a muddy footprint on the rug beside his bed. He peered at it and frowned. Odd, he thought, as he slowly lowered the lid of the box.

14. Prisoner!

The next day Samuel was up early, before the rest of Dunadd were awake. He closed the door of the cottage behind him and stepped out into the icy-cold silence of the moor. It was quiet outside the cottage. No one else was about, except of course old Mr Hughes, attempting to clear the new snow that had fallen overnight.

"Where are you off to at this time in the morning?" the old man asked.

"Oh, nowhere special. Just out for a walk."

"Oh aye? All this fresh air's getting to you, lad," he remarked with a knowing smile. "Don't be getting up to mischief again, and setting the women to worry. We had enough of that last night."

Samuel smiled and promised he wouldn't, then set off down the driveway, under the frozen beech trees, hoping no one would notice him from the rows of gleaming windows.

He remembered standing with Fiona in the corridor last night as she whispered "Meet me at the waterfall." She knew the quickest way to Lynns Farm and would take him there. It was important to speak to Mr MacFarlane, and hear what he had to say.

Samuel whistled to himself as he walked beneath the snow-clad trees. His breath froze as soon as it left his body. He crossed the narrow lane, and vaulted the gate into the fields below. He sank to his knees in deep snow, and struggled to make his way down into the gully by walking on the top of the snowdrifts. A milky white mist was just lifting off the hills, and the peaks of distant mountains broke through like islands in a sea. They shone pink and purple in the strange early morning light. It was amazing how half of the moor could be bathed in sunlight, while the other was still cloaked in shadow. It was part of the beauty of the place. The mist created an illusion. If you didn't know better, Samuel thought, you would think there was a lake down there, lapping at the edges of the moor like a distant shore.

He heard the waterfall before he saw it, and made his way towards it. Curtains of frozen ice were caught in its flow, fringed with gleaming icicles. It was a startling sight, and he stared at it for some moments, transfixed. Fiona hadn't arrived yet, so he waited for her, listening to the sound of the water travelling under the ice. Normally the roar of the waterfall was deafening, but much of it was frozen over, held back, caught in mid-motion.

A weak winter sun rose above the mist, and still no one appeared. For no reason that he could explain, Samuel began to feel nervous, as if he was being watched. He looked around him at the high ridges, half-expecting to see the ghosts of slaughtered infantry men appear above him.

He glanced at his watch. It was strange of Fiona not to be on time. She'd probably slept in, or else she'd forgotten all about their meeting — although he knew in his heart of hearts that wouldn't really be like Fiona. She was as keen as he was to continue their investigation.

Suddenly a sound caught his attention. A small pebble had been dropped into the water from a great height. He looked up. There, on a high ridge way above him stood a dark figure in the snow. Samuel's heart sank. It was Charles.

"Waiting for someone?" he shouted, above the sound of the water. "She won't be coming, I'm afraid. I've made sure of that."

Then Charles jumped down from his high perch above the waterfall, and made his way round to where Samuel stood. Samuel watched him in silence, refusing to be drawn.

"Thought you'd meet up with my little sister then, did you? On the sly?"

"Why does it bother you so much?"

Charles stepped closer to him and said "I don't like strangers poking around. I heard what you were up to last night, by the way." Samuel remembered the door quietly closing. "Thought you'd go and see the old man at Lynns farm, did you? I wouldn't advise it. He doesn't like unexpected guests."

"We're not doing anything wrong," Samuel said. "We just want to find out more about the house. Its history ..."

"Is that right?"

Charles eyed him angrily. "That man keeps a shotgun in his barn, and you want to take my sister there? Don't you think my mother might have something to say about that?"

"We'd be careful," Samuel protested.

"Careful?" Charles laughed. "If you were careful you wouldn't even think about going there."

"Why? What's so terrible about the place?"

"It's not the place. It's the man," Sebastian added quietly. He had appeared behind Samuel now, to join forces with his brother.

"We're just trying to protect our sister," Charles said.

"From what?"

But Charles just looked at Samuel. No one knew what burdens he had to carry in silence, not even his own brother. He wasn't about to tell a complete stranger about them, an outsider, a newcomer.

"One little reminder," he went on. "You may think you're nice and cosy living in that cottage, but one word from me, and I could get her to evict you, just like that."

"What is it you're so afraid of?" Samuel said, looking him in the eye.

Charles's face was white and he looked haunted, as if Samuel's words had struck true.

"Just keep away from our sister. Okay?"

"Where is she?" Samuel asked now.

Suddenly Charles grinned wolfishly in a way that Samuel had never seen before, and held up a key in his hand. He dangled it in front of Samuel's face. "Learning a lesson," he said. "Learning to accept that her brothers know what's best for her."

Samuel's chest tightened with panic. "Where is she?" he cried again, "You can't have locked her up!"

But just as he was about to grab Charles' arm Charles pushed him backwards, knocking him to the ground. The shock of it took Samuel's breath away. He lay winded for a time, before gradually struggling to his feet.

The brothers had turned and fled, leaving him alone beside the waterfall.

As Charles and Sebastian hurried away up the hillside towards Dunadd, Charles suddenly stopped in his tracks, as if frozen to the spot. His breath was coming in rasps. A vision filled his head, like a flashback or memory from a time before. All he could see were the sweating flanks of a large black horse pounding across the turf towards the hidden ravine where the waterfall lay. He could hear the animal snorting with the effort, flecks of foam flying from its bit and bridle as it galloped. Its unknown rider urged it on, but

Charles couldn't see the rider. He could only make out the horse, see its sweat and hear its effort as it surged ahead. It was a glimpse only, and then just as suddenly the vision was gone, leaving Charles confused as he stood there in the snow.

His brother looked at him in alarm.

"What's wrong?"

"I ... I don't know ... Nothing," Charles stammered. He slowly shook his head free of the vision, and the pair made their way back to the house.

Samuel looked around him desperately, at the frozen-white curtain of water and the high ridges of the gully surrounding him. He had to get back to Dunadd and tell Mrs Morton what the boys had done to Fiona. But then he froze. They were her sons. She would never believe him. It was their word against his.

He thought about this as he made his way up the steep hillside beside the waterfall. It was hard work, climbing through the snow. The moor, which had seemed so beautiful only moments before, was now a hostile environment. He no longer noticed the magical quality of the mist on the lower plain, or the cerulean blue of the sky against the whiteness of snow. Nothing else mattered but the pain and exhaustion in his body, and the need to find Fiona.

Finally, when he reached the road, he stopped to rest against the gatepost, trying to get his breath back. His thoughts were with his friend. How could her own brothers do that to her, lock her up somewhere? Back at Dunadd he ran into the big house, his feet pounding noisily along the empty corridors, calling out her name, but there seemed to be no one about. Granny Hughes was not in her usual place, scolding the world in general and doing the dishes.

Instead he found Mrs Morton sitting at the kitchen table drinking a cup of coffee, stroking Lettice the rabbit who had hopped off the table into her lap. She looked alarmed at Samuel's outburst.

"Whatever's the matter?" she said.

"Fiona," he cried, out of breath. "She's locked up somewhere. Charles and Sebastian did it."

There was a long silence.

"I've already spoken to Charles, Samuel. He told me what you were planning to do. I warned you not to go anywhere near Lynns Farm. If you disobey me again, and lead Fiona into trouble as well, I shall have to take serious action."

"But they've locked up Fiona," he spluttered. "I saw the key."

"Don't be ridiculous," she snapped, looking irritated for the first time. "My sons might do many things I disapprove of, but they do not, as a rule, lock up their sister. Fiona went out early this morning," she went on. "She's off enjoying herself somewhere, and has promised to be back by lunchtime."

"But where?" he cried, beginning to despair.

Mrs Morton shook her head. "Where she usually goes. All those secret haunts of yours."

Samuel spun round and left the room. He knew there was no point in talking to Mrs Morton. She would never believe his word against her two sons.

He ran down the corridor and out into the courtyard.

He stood on the lawn in front of Dunadd. A thick white blanket of freshly-fallen snow lay across it, but there were new tracks, as if someone had recently passed that way. The boating pond, he thought in a flash of inspiration. He followed the tracks along the tree-lined path.

The pond was still frozen over. He stepped onto the jetty and walked to the end of it. The blue rowing boat was trapped in ice, untouched. No one had been able to use it in weeks.

Suddenly, in the stillness, he heard a sound, very faint at first, but then more distinct. It was the sound of someone crying. At first he wondered if it was the Weeping Woman, come to haunt him even here, but he quickly realized it couldn't be. This was a different sound, less sad, and it was accompanied by an angry knocking noise. Someone was knocking and banging against the wooden door of the summer house on the other side of the water.

He leapt to his feet and ran round the pond, calling out Fiona's name as he did so. He had no key but pressed his ear to the locked door.

"Is that you, Samuel?" she called in a muffled voice. "For God's sake, get me out of here."

"Wait there," he said.

"As if I can do anything else!" she called back, as he disappeared behind the summer house where a barbecue and a tin box of supplies were kept. He reappeared with a long metal bar, and broke open the lock.

"Wait till I get my hands on those brothers of mine," Fiona spat. "They tricked me — they told me you'd come up here ..."

"There's something strange about all this," Samuel murmured. "Charles doesn't usually carry on like this, does he?"

Fiona shrugged. "I don't know. He's frightened."

"But what of?"

The two of them were silent.

"They warned me off going to Lynns Farm," Samuel said.

"How did they ...?"

"They must have been listening last night, when we fixed it up. I thought I saw someone ... And not only that," Samuel added, "but your mother knows about it too. They told her."

Fiona's face fell. "How can we go to Lynns Farm now?"

"You try and stop me."

15. Lynns Farm

Upstairs in the tower Charles sat on his bed, his head in his hands. Down at the waterfall something strange had happened to him, but he didn't know what. He kept seeing the image of a horse pounding towards the ravine, its muscular black flanks sweating with the effort. He didn't understand any of it; he was confused, but he knew that something was terribly wrong. He felt strangely frightened.

And what had compelled him to lock his sister in the summer house?

He thought again of his father's letter and the dreams that came to disturb him at night. He needed to confide in someone, anyone. He couldn't carry this burden alone. It was too much. But who could he tell? There was no one. No one would understand ...

When Samuel and Fiona got back to Dunadd, far from being pleased to see them, Mrs Morton was furious and told Fiona she would not be allowed out for a week.

"I know what you've been up to, Fiona. The boys have told me. I don't want you going anywhere near that place, do you hear me? Nor Samuel for that matter either."

"Why not?" Fiona cried. "What's wrong with Mr MacFarlane?"

"He's a bitter cantankerous old man, that's what. He's unpleasant and rude and a troublemaker. I must say that when I agreed to let the Cunninghams rent the cottage, I didn't realize Samuel would give us this much trouble."

"But he hasn't," Fiona protested. "It's Charles. He's making you believe his lies."

"That's enough Fiona."

"But Samuel is my friend!"

Mrs Morton softened slightly. "All this nonsense has to stop. Samuel has to learn to get along with the boys, without all these arguments."

"He has tried. It's Charles who doesn't like him."

"I won't have you telling tales, Fiona."

"But it's true!"

"That's enough!"

"If you say so!" Fiona scowled, and stomped off to her room to brood.

"That's exactly where you should be, madam!" Chris Morton shouted after her daughter. "You need some time alone to think about the consequences of your actions. And there'll be no more jaunts with Samuel for a while."

But her sons did not get off lightly either. Having dealt with Fiona, she rounded on them angrily.

"And you two needn't stand there smirking. Locking your sister up in the summer house in these freezing conditions. Have you any idea how dangerous that could have been? When were you planning to let her out?" Her fury knew no bounds. It was a very black household that day, with everyone banished to their rooms and Chris Morton looking as sour-faced as Samuel had ever seen her. He decided to make himself scarce. It felt as if the whole of Dunadd lay under a dark cloud, and he wondered if it was his fault. Everyone had been getting on fine before he came along. Now everything was ruined.

Back at the cottage Isabel watched him as he took off his boots in the narrow flagged kitchen.

"Things not exactly going well between you and the boys at the moment?"

Samuel shrugged. "You could say that!"

"Try to be patient with them," she murmured. "They'll come round eventually."

"I have been patient. I mean, I am being."

She sighed. "There's something bothering those boys." She put her book down on the arm of the sofa. "Maybe it's something to do with their father's death."

"Is that *my* fault?"

"No, but ..." she looked out of the window, and sighed again. "If only it would stop snowing long enough for the roads to clear. Then we could get you all off to school. It's like a pressure cooker at the moment. You just need some distraction."

"S'pose," he mumbled, disappearing down the corridor to his room.

Isabel stared after him. *Being his usual communicative self,* she thought as she stared into the heart of the stove.

Samuel felt wretched and lonely. Fiona was not allowed out to see him, and he missed her badly. He had no one to discuss it all with, the questions and thoughts that were buzzing around his head. He still had the ebony box in his possession, the worn leather bag, the ring and the tartan safely stowed away inside it, along with the pages of the journal. What if the Mortons suspected something, and realized it had gone missing from its usual place in the library? Did they even know about it? Samuel wasn't sure. There had been so much dust on the lid when he first discovered the box that it looked as if it hadn't been touched in years. He thought about going down to visit Lynns Farm on his own, without Fiona, but he couldn't do that. He would just have to wait until he could arrange to see her again.

Later that afternoon, as he was collecting firewood

for the stove, he heard a footstep behind him and spun round. He thought at first it might be Fiona, but Sebastian was standing there, looking sheepish.

"What do *you* want?" Samuel said.

"Look, I'm really sorry about what happened at the waterfall, you know."

Samuel turned his back, and continued to pick up firewood.

"It's a pity we can't all just be friends, really," Sebastian went on.

"That's rich," Samuel muttered. "Coming from you."

Sebastian looked awkward. "I suppose that did come out a big wrong. Look, I just wanted to say ... Charles gets so worked up about things, that's all."

"I've noticed!" Then he looked Sebastian in the eye. "Why do you always do what he says all the time?"

Sebastian lowered his eyes. "He's my brother. He gets easily offended."

"So you let him bully you?"

"It's not like that."

"What is it like then?" Samuel asked. "I just don't get it."

Sebastian sighed. "Charles doesn't trust anyone. He's frightened all the time. Our father's death, and the way he died, well, it frightens him. If I turned against him as well, he'd never get over it."

"He would," Samuel said. "In time. People always do. Anyway, you can't let him bully you all your life."

Sebastian ignored this. "He's right about the farm, though. You shouldn't go there alone. Or with Fiona. It's dangerous."

Samuel turned away from him.

"You're not going to do anything stupid, are you?" Sebastian added. "Like try to go to Lynns Farm on your own?"

"Of course not," Samuel lied. But he was making his plans. If Fiona wasn't allowed out to see him, he would have to go alone.

"Looks like we might be able to get you to school soon," Isabel remarked later that day, glancing out of the window.

Samuel looked up, his heart sinking.

"School?" he said.

"Yes. You remember. That building with classrooms? I've been listening to the radio. Looks like a thaw might set in before the end of the week. Thank God! I'm beginning to forget what the rest of the world looks like."

Samuel looked crestfallen.

"It'll be good for you," she went on. "You'll make new friends. It'll take your mind off things." By "things" she was clearly referring to his troubles with Charles and Sebastian. She didn't know all of the details — Chris Morton had not spoken to her about it yet — but she could make an intelligent guess as to how things stood.

So their long winter of isolation was coming to an end. And perhaps he would never have time to find out the truth about Catherine Morton after all.

Samuel was sitting in his room the next morning, trying to read. He couldn't concentrate, his mind wouldn't focus. Suddenly, there was a knocking sound on his window. He sat up on the bed and saw Fiona's face peering in at him from beneath a brightly-striped woolly hat.

"Quick. Let me in!" she mouthed through the glass. He flung open the window, and a pile of powdery-dry snow fell into his room.

"Help me up," she grunted, as she hauled herself in over the window sill.

"I thought you were grounded!"

"I am, but I couldn't stand it any more. We're going to Lynns Farm today, and that's that. I've made up my mind. You weren't thinking of going on your own, were you?" she added then, glancing at him suspiciously.

"Of course not," Samuel said.

"Because I'd hate to think I was missing out on anything. And anyway, it wouldn't be safe on your own."

"I know. That's what I was thinking. That's why the thought never crossed my mind."

Her eyes narrowed, and she cuffed him round the head.

"What was that for?"

"It's good to see you again," was all she said.

Samuel grinned. "You too."

"If Mum finds out I'm missing, I'll be in big trouble."

"She can't keep you locked up forever."

"I don't know. My family are good at that. Listen, if we want to go to Lynns Farm, I reckon we should go now."

They kept to the trees as they made their way down to the waterfall. They crossed the lane, and then climbed the wide five-bar gate into the fields beyond. The wind still carried the sting of the arctic in it, and their faces froze.

The roar of water travelling beneath ice met their ears. The Wharry Burn had cut a rocky gorge into the hillside at this point, and they avoided this, knowing how dangerous it could be for a person who didn't know the moor well. In the deep snow you could walk right off the precipice without realizing it was there.

Fiona kept glancing nervously over her shoulder. "What if anyone's followed us?"

"They won't."

"You're right," she said, trying to take courage. "Besides, they wouldn't dare do that to me again." When Samuel saw her blue eyes flash with fury like that, he could believe it.

"You're really scary when you're angry, did you know that?" Samuel murmured.

They skirted the side of the ravine, and slid down the sloping bank beside the waterfall.

They went right to the water's edge, beneath the waterfall itself, and stared up at it.

Samuel thought of the last time he had been here. He shivered with cold.

"Can you believe we sometimes swim here, in the summer?" Fiona said.

"Imagine doing that now!"

"No thanks!"

Around them the land rose up steeply so that they were in a dip of the moor, surrounded on all sides by high ridges, almost like a room with walls. Samuel kept looking up as he had done last time, half-expecting to see soldiers or figures on the crest of the hill, or more likely her brothers re-appearing.

"It's strange how I always feel watched here," he said, looking around. "There's something about this place."

"This is where the Government army camped the night before the battle," Fiona said. "There's an atmosphere here, isn't there?"

Samuel looked up at the high ridges and nodded.

"And what was it all for?" she went on. Neither side had claimed a victory in the end. After a day of pointless fighting and massive loss of life, the Duke of Argyll didn't even bother to turn up the next day to renew the fighting. His men simply drifted off, unwilling to fight another day.

Fiona bent down and kicked aside the snow to reveal a ring of stones that had formed the site of an old campfire.

"That was us last summer, before you moved in," she said. "Me and the boys camped out here one night. We had a fire and cooked sausages. It was great fun." She looked sad for a moment, as if she was remembering a time when she had got on better with her brothers than she did at the moment. Something had come between them. Life had soured at Dunadd.

"It's my fault, isn't it?" Samuel said, looking guilty.

He couldn't help thinking that the three Morton children had been wandering this moor for years before he came along. They were born here, and knew no other life. This was everything to them, everything they had ever known.

Fiona shook her head. "This place is a million times better since you came."

But still she looked sad about her brothers.

"Are we going to visit this Lynns Farm or not?" she said, goading them into action.

"Should we have phoned first?" Samuel said as they followed the course of the Wharry Burn. "Let him know we're coming? After all, your mother says he's a bitter, cantankerous old man."

"It's probably best he doesn't know. We'll just turn up."

"That's true. And if he doesn't like it, we leave."

"And the shotgun?" Fiona added, almost jokingly.

"We'll worry about that one later."

They looked up at the horizon where a weak winter sun was climbing steadily into the sky. Lynns Farm lay somewhere beyond the waterfall, in a hollow, so that it was impossible to see it at all from the road.

As they made their way beside the burn, a figure watched them from above. Had they turned their heads they would have seen him standing there, dark against the snow. Charles watched them, and again he suffered the strange vision he'd seen earlier, like a flashback or some long-buried memory from a time before. A horse with an unknown rider, pounding its way towards the ravine ...

The waters of the Wharry Burn babbled and gurgled beneath the ice, as Fiona and Samuel made their way into the gully.

Finally the farmhouse came into view, a small low-lying whitewashed building with several chimneys and low eaves. It lay in shadow, as if the sun rarely got this far beyond the trees. No birds sang. It seemed a very dark and secretive place, as if no postman, milkman or delivery van ever came here.

The farmyard looked neglected and deserted, broken bits of machinery and farm equipment lay around, unused. The windows of the house were blank and staring, and Fiona and Samuel surveyed the gloomy scene in silence, wondering what to do next. They left the cover of the trees and began to walk forward. They had to pluck up courage to cross the empty yard towards the house, in full view of those windows. Suddenly a big black vicious-looking dog emerged from an open door and hurled itself towards them, snarling and gnashing its teeth. It was yanked back on its chain, having run as far as it could. The children stood rooted to the spot.

The figure of an elderly man appeared from the shadows, and squinted his eyes to see what the noise was about.

"Quiet, dog," he growled in a low voice, and the dog instantly fell silent.

The two groups regarded each other in silence across the empty farmyard.

The man spoke first. "What do you want?"

"We're from Dunadd. The house up on the hill?"

The man looked at them suspiciously. "Oh aye? And what are you doing here?"

"We came to see a Mr MacFarlane."

"You're looking at 'im."

"Oh good. You see, we ... we've come for a reason ..."

"Have ye now?" was all he said in reply.

"We need to talk to you."

"What about?"

"Well, it's a bit difficult really ..." Samuel began.

"Ach, it's not that mother of yours again? Thinks she owns the whole moor. Well, I'm tellin' ye now, she doesn't own this bit of it."

Fiona cut in, deciding it was best to get straight to the point. "My mother doesn't know we're here, Mr MacFarlane. We have a ghost at Dunadd, a weeping woman who paces the corridors." Mr MacFarlane appeared to be listening intently. "Samuel has heard her, and a figure has been seen up at the windows of Dunadd."

"Aye. I've seen her."

Fiona and Samuel stared at him.

"When?"

"When the family's been away in the past. At first I wondered if it was maybe Mrs Hughes cleaning. The figure just stands there at the drawing room windows, a woman in a long blue gown."

"That's her," Samuel said.

"We found some pages of a journal belonging to a girl called Catherine Morton."

The old man looked up, his eyes glinting. He seemed intrigued by this.

"And a little leather bag in our library," Fiona went on, "an old relic of some kind which we thought might be connected to her. It contained a ring wrapped in a piece of Jacobite tartan."

Mr MacFarlane didn't seem at all surprised by this news, and merely nodded. "You'd better come in," and he led the way into his dark farmhouse, into a low-roofed kitchen with blackened beams on the ceiling.

They pulled up chairs at a big wooden table, and Mr MacFarlane proceeded to fill a kettle for tea.

"So it's the past ye're wanting to dig up now, is it? To find out some of the secrets they don't discuss at Dunadd? I guess that after all these years you Mortons had been hoping they'd be forgotten, hey?"

"Forgotten? What secrets?"

Mr MacFarlane sighed and said: "You've never heard about it then? Aye, I wondered ...." He took a deep breath. "It's a love story, I suppose. A tragic tale. A Morton woman from Dunadd fell in love with a MacFarlane from Lynns Farm about three hundred years ago. It could only end in tragedy of course, and that's exactly what happened."

"I've never heard this story before," Fiona said uncertainly.

Mr MacFarlane gave a bitter laugh. "Have ye not?"

He laughed again. "Ach, well, I suppose it's only to be expected."

"What is?"

"It's what the Mortons would have wanted, for the story to disappear without trace, but your weeping woman wouldn't leave them alone. She cannit rest until her story is resolved and the family make amends."

"Amends for what?" Fiona cried, confused.

"For forbidding her to love a common farmer, and killing her into the bargain."

A shocked silence fell, and Mr MacFarlane turned his back on them and began to pour boiling water into a teapot.

"Does my mother know about this?" Fiona repeated dumbly.

Mr MacFarlane watched her in silence.

"What type of a ring was it you found?" he asked instead.

"It's silver, twisted into a lover's knot, with a Celtic pattern engraved on it. Very simple and beautiful."

He nodded again, sagely. "Aye, that's the one." Then he poured cups of tea and took his place at the table with a great sigh.

"So you found a journal then?"

"Not the whole thing. We found some pages torn from it. It was written by a twelve-year-old girl, Catherine Morton."

Mr MacFarlane shook his head in amazement. "That's her! I never knew there was a journal," he whispered in awe. "I'd like to see it, if I may?"

Fiona and Samuel nodded, relieved that the old man was proving to be not nearly as terrifying as they'd imagined. "There's a story in my family, passed down through the generations," he began. "An ancestor of mine in 1714 or thereabouts, fell in love with a Morton woman from the Dunadd estate. She was Catherine, the youngest child of the laird, Sir Charles Morton. Patrick MacFarlane worked as a stable boy at Dunadd and they'd become close as children, running about the moor together all day long, to the horror of Catherine's parents. When they grew up, they fell in love."

"What happened to them?" Samuel asked.

"The Mortons found out, and she was punished."

"How was she punished?" Fiona asked timidly.

"She was locked up in Dunadd, prevented from ever leaving the house again, even for a breath of fresh air. Before that the pair used to meet in secret on the moor. They were married secretly by the waterfall. Patrick gave her the ring and swore they would be together one day and live on Sheriffmuir, enjoying it like they always had as children. Ach, well, life wasn't as simple as all that. Catherine had two very headstrong brothers who helped to enforce their father's will. They followed her one day to their secret meeting place by the waterfall. She was dragged home to Dunadd, and Patrick was severely beaten."

"As the brothers dragged Catherine away, Patrick called after her that he would see her again. But a few weeks later the Jacobite uprising of 1715 swept the country. It led to a battle on this very moor, as you know. Catherine was desperate to see Patrick one last time, but she was locked in the house. The Mortons, of course, supported the opposing side. They helped billet some of Argyll's officers, supplying them with food and hay for their horses.

"Patrick made up his mind to fight alongside the Highlanders on 13th November, wearing his Jacobite tartan. Catherine watched the battle from an upstairs window, including the slaughter of the Highlanders. Her own Patrick died in the fighting. The silver ring you mention has its own story to tell, for when the brothers separated the pair of lovers, one of them then withdrew the silver ring from her finger and threw it down in the mud. Patrick retrieved it and carried it with him into the field of battle — for luck, although it brought him none."

A silence fell in the small dark kitchen, over the three silent figures at the table.

"The story goes that a servant who was sympathetic to the pair searched for Patrick's body among the dead, and brought back his dagger and a piece of his tartan. He also found the ring which Patrick had tried unsuccessfully to bury as he lay wounded and dying on the battlefield. It lay beside his outstretched fingers, and the servant saw it shining in the dirt. The dagger was returned to Patrick's mother and kept in the family. The ring and the piece of tartan were delivered into Catherine's hands, together with the information that he had died a brave and courageous death." Mr MacFarlane sighed and looked into the shadows before continuing with his story. "She grieved for another two months, through a long and terrible winter, and then, on 13th January 1716, exactly two months to the day after the Battle of Sheriffmuir, she died giving birth to a premature boy. The baby was stillborn."

Fiona and Samuel sat without moving, in stunned silence, horrified.

But Mr MacFarlane had not quite finished his tale. "It was sometimes said that Catherine died cursing the male line of her family, swearing she'd make sure her father and brothers would be punished for what they'd done to her. She died full of bitterness and anger."

There was a short silence, as they sat thinking sadly of the unhappy pair.

"There were three sons living on Lynns Farm at that time. I am descended from Patrick's brother, the only one to survive the battle. He inherited the farm from his mother, married, had children and died in his bed at the age of eighty. He told the story of his brother's doomed love to his own children, and made sure it was passed down through the generations, as a warning against having anything to do with a Morton. That's how I know."

Mr MacFarlane sat looking at the two children, who were shocked into silence, and he felt a little sorry for them. "So you'd never heard tell of any of this up at Dunadd? It's a well-known story hereabouts."

"My parents never said anything about it!"

He nodded. "Perhaps they were trying to protect you. It's a tragic tale for young ears to hear, right enough," he said in a low voice. "Ach, I'm sorry you had to hear it."

Fiona shook her head. "No. No, it's best we did. Perhaps we can make amends, like you said, help put her ghost to rest by resolving the sufferings of the past."

Mr MacFarlane looked at her kindly and said "The past is never resolved, my dear. It just is."

"But ghosts can be laid to rest," Samuel insisted.

"Drink up yer tea, son," the old man said sadly, "before it gets cauld."

Before they left, Fiona wanted to ask one last thing. "Why does my mother not speak to you, Mr MacFarlane?"

He looked at her and his eyes twinkled. "Apart from the past, you mean? Aye, well ... various reasons."

He sighed, and shifted in his chair. "The main one being, I didn't want the story of Catherine Morton to be forgotten. I thought she deserved to be remembered. A historian once came sniffing around here after local ghost stories. A nice woman, she was. Wanted to include the particulars in an archive in the Museum of Scotland. Thought it would make interesting reading for later generations."

The children listened, wide-eyed. "So I told her exactly what I've just told you, and she kept a record of it. It's there in the museum archives apparently, if anyone wants to see." He lowered his gaze then. "Your mother didn't agree. She didn't want people to think that Dunadd has a ghost. She wanted to let sleeping dogs lie, and for the memory of Catherine Morton to fade."

"Why?" Fiona said, staring at him intently.

The old man tried to avoid her eye. "Well now, a mother will always try to protect her young, will she not?"

Fiona still looked perplexed. Mr MacFarlane turned solemn for a moment.

"How do you think it would make Charles and Sebastian feel, if they knew about the story of the curse?" he said gently. "Would they still lead happy lives afterwards, do you think?"

Fiona sat still, while the significance of his words sank in. Then she stood up abruptly. "It's just a story," she murmured. "No one can prove it."

Mr MacFarlane drank his tea thoughtfully, and said nothing more.

16. Face at the Window

As they walked away from the farm, Samuel cast sidelong glances in Fiona's direction. She walked with her head down, trying to digest what Mr MacFarlane had told them. He knew she was having trouble accepting what they'd just heard.

Samuel felt frustrated. They had solved the mystery of who their weeping woman was. She and the twelve-year-old Catherine Morton of the journal were one and the same, as they had always suspected, but they were no nearer to ridding Dunadd of her sad presence.

"Look, Samuel, let's just face it," Fiona snapped. "She's not going to go away." As they neared the waterfall they could hear the rush of the water tumbling beneath the snow and ice. Samuel was about to make a sharp retort, but thought better of it. He knew she was upset, and he could understand that. If he'd just found out that a curse had been placed on his family, he probably wouldn't have been particularly pleased about it either.

"Maybe we just have to learn to live with her," Fiona added wistfully. "Perhaps she'll always be part of Dunadd."

"In one sense, yes," he murmured, "but I still think we could help her in some way."

"I can't believe my mum never said anything about this. She knew all along, and didn't say a word."

Samuel was quiet. All they could hear was the sound of the Wharry Burn. "You can't blame her really!"

"What?" Fiona glared at him.

"Maybe she's worried."

Fiona looked blank. "Oh come on, Fiona. You heard what Mr MacFarlane said, about the curse she put on your family?"

She shook her head. "That's just a story. Mr MacFarlane said so himself. Just because she died an angry woman, that doesn't mean to say it has any effect on us now. Anyway, it's not even true. Not all of the men in my family died young." She hesitated, looking disturbed. "They couldn't have, otherwise the Mortons would have died out long ago. It's just a stupid story." She was getting angry now.

"Yes, but what about your father?"

"What about him?" Fiona's mood darkened.

"He died young, didn't he? Before his time?"

"It's just a coincidence," Fiona said in a small frightened voice.

Samuel paused for a moment. "What if it isn't?" he whispered.

Neither of them wanted to think about the consequences of that. Overhead, a solitary bird let out a desolate cry. They walked on, their heads bent low.

"Poor Catherine Morton." Fiona shuddered. "She was the youngest of three children, with two older brothers." There was a pause. "Just like me." Fiona and Samuel looked at one another.

"Do you ever have the feeling," Samuel murmured, "that history is repeating itself? That we're acting out something that has already happened before?"

"How do you mean?" Fiona said in a low voice, although she already knew what he meant.

"Nothing. It's just that ... it's almost like we're all being programmed to re-enact stuff from the past. Me, you, Charles and Sebastian. They dragged you away and locked you in the summer house, just like the Morton brothers of long ago ... it's almost like we can't help ourselves."

"And that's why Charles and Seb are behaving the way they are, you mean? That it's part of this ..." she struggled with the word, "curse thing."

Samuel shrugged. "It's a possibility." There was silence for a minute, as they made their way up hill towards the white tower of Dunadd in the distance, with its long ranks of gleaming windows. There was a low mist coming down over the trees of Dunadd again, closing the place in. Patches of mist caught between the branches, and drifted close to the windows. "She died a bitter and angry woman, that's what he said. You can almost feel it in the air. I wonder where she's buried?"

Fiona shrugged. "With the rest of the Mortons I suppose."

"Where's that?"

"In the cemetery, down in the village. We have our own private chapel there and a family vault."

Samuel lifted his head and surveyed the scene before him. "Maybe she's not with the rest of the family. Maybe she's here at Dunadd, the only Morton to be buried on Sheriffmuir."

"Why would she be?"

"I don't know, it's just an idea."

"So what are we going to do? Start digging?" she asked sarcastically.

"We could ask Mr MacFarlane. Maybe he would know. I'd like to see him again, anyway."

That afternoon Samuel stroked the dark ebony box on his desk under the window. Its surface was so intricately carved that it was knobbly to touch.

He opened it, took out the leather bag and examined the silver ring and the piece of tartan by the light of the window. The ring shone, barely tarnished at all despite its great age. As Mr MacFarlane said, if it could speak, it would have its own story to tell. It had gone with Patrick into the field of battle, and lay, half-covered with dirt, as the wounded lay dying all around him. Then it had been found and restored to Catherine, who had died and left her treasures locked up in a precious box. Who had thought to keep them safe all these years? Who had placed the things in the box, and then placed the box safely away in the library, to be forgotten and to acquire layers of dust until years later? Was it Catherine's mother, the mother one never hears anything about, who lived in the shadow of a domineering husband and her equally domineering sons? Who knew?

Samuel lay the leaf-brown pages of the journal on his desk, and read the faded handwriting. Her words came at him out of the past.

My brothers are not the most patient and mild-mannered of people, but I know how to handle them ...

For my birthday I was given this booke, a leather-bound volume. Mother taught me to read and write, and she considers it will be good for me to keepe a journal ...

Father is ... well, Father is Father.

I respect him, but I keepe my distance. I'm learning to blend in to my surroundings.

I'm free when I'm up on the muir. As wild as my brothers. As long as Father sees naught.

Mrs Fletcher says that Mother has new-fangled ideas in teaching a wee slip of a lass to read and write, and that my father would strongly disapprove if he knew. So I make as if not to draw attention to myself and pretend ignorance as necesserie. Tis better this way.

And then he read about her friendship with Patrick.

He listens to me as if I have something important to say. (At home I am mostly ignored, and ridiculed by my brothers if I dare to offer an opinion).

A twelve-year-old girl learning to cope in a household full of domineering men, trying to keep her head down, suppress her own intelligence. And a mother, Lady Cecilia, who no doubt lived to regret the way her daughter was treated. A story was beginning to emerge. A very personal story, with not one but two sad women at its centre, Catherine Morton and her mother, Lady Cecilia. Catherine was a girl who had dared to defy the rules of the world in which she lived. And she had paid a terrible price. Her brothers had thought of her as a witch at times, and she had been happy for them to think that.

After Catherine's death, someone had kept these precious objects safe, the ring and the piece of tartan, and the ebony box she had treasured so. These things were tokens of the couple's love for one another. It occurred to Samuel then that maybe they could eradicate the curse after all. They could use these things in any ceremony they might perform, as a way of burying the two together, or trying, at least, to put them to rest.

He thought about Catherine's mother, Lady Cecilia. Had she grieved secretly for her lost daughter, lost in so many ways? Perhaps she too had paced the upstairs rooms, weeping long after her daughter's death, blaming herself for what happened to her daughter.

He thought about the two lost souls, Catherine Morton and Patrick MacFarlane, who had befriended one another despite their differences. He thought of her pacing the corridors and weeping as the battle raged on the fields below; how she had watched the terrible slaughter, both sides devastated in the attack. A battle with no victors. Then he thought of the baby, born too early to survive, and how Catherine's suffering had been inflicted by her own father and brothers. He gently gathered together the papers from the journal, and replaced them in the ebony box. He was determined to help her to rest in peace.

On a sudden impulse Samuel went outside and made his way to the front of Dunadd. He looked up at the big windows of the drawing room. He wasn't expecting to see anything particularly, but there she was. A figure at the window, a white face looking down at him, a sad face framed by dark hair. She wore a long navy-blue plaid gown, and now that he could see her more clearly, he realized that she did look younger than he had first thought. Bitterness had aged her prematurely perhaps in those weeks before her death. He gazed upwards. There seemed to be a knowing look on her face, as if she knew that he was standing out there on the lawn, and what he was thinking.

She fixed him with her dark eyes, nodded, and then turned away.

17. A Small, Silver Dagger

Fiona sat alone in front of the drawing room fire, brooding. Mr Hughes had stacked the huge hearth with logs, and all she had to do was put a match to it. The flames danced on the hearth rug.

When Chris Morton walked in, she found her daughter sitting there, quite motionless in the shadows.

"No lights on?" she asked and bent to switch on a lamp or two. At once the objects in the room sprang into sharp relief, and the darkness shrank back into the corners.

Fiona looked at her mother angrily.

"We went to Mr MacFarlane's house today," she began.

Mrs Morton straightened up. "Why did you do that?"

But Fiona didn't let her finish. "He told us about the weeping woman, about Catherine Morton and what happened to her."

Her mother fell silent. No longer bustling about and bossing her daughter, she was at a loss for words.

"Did you know about this story?" Fiona demanded.

Mrs Morton hesitated, then sighed.

"Of course I knew about it."

"Why didn't you tell us?"

"I didn't want to frighten you."

"Charles and Seb ... do they know?"

Chris Morton shook her head. "I don't think so."

Then she sat down in a chair, her shoulders slumped.

"I'm sick of that old man interfering. He has no right ... It's all very well for him to repeat it verbatim as if it's some piece of interesting local history ... It might be just a story to him, but to us it's more than that. I just want people to forget ... and then maybe it will be all right again."

Fiona watched her mother sadly. "It will be all right, Mum," she murmured, more gently than she intended, and Chris Morton looked at her daughter in surprise.

Upstairs in their tower rooms, Charles and Sebastian waited like everyone else for the big freeze to be over, and for a thaw to set in. It was as if Sheriffmuir lay under a spell of some kind. Charles sat at his computer, his eyes dark with thoughts he couldn't put a name to.

He was reaching a difficult age, Mrs Morton speculated, trying to reassure herself, but the truth was, he hadn't seemed like himself lately. He was moody and stubborn, "off colour" as Granny Hughes politely put it. But it was more than that. He was always sullen, preoccupied. Something was on his mind. He watched Samuel and his sister darkly, as if they were his sworn enemies. It was as if he couldn't help himself. His mother was beginning to suspect that she had been right after all, that this was not a healthy atmosphere for them to grow up in. She had tried to tell herself that it was, but the memory of that night when her husband died was always coming back to her — the scream she heard in the library, and then finding him stretched out on the floor like that. And the shadow she'd seen slip from the room out the corner of her eye. And the letter she'd found on the desk, a letter her husband had only just finished writing. She'd wanted to destroy it, but hadn't felt able to in the end, so she had buried it in one of the drawers, amongst all the loose bits of paper that she never had the time or energy to sort out, trying to pretend it didn't exist. It was so much easier to keep things as they were, to refuse to change anything.

Perhaps she should get rid of the place, after all, simply sell up and start anew elsewhere. But the thought of all those years of history — family history, her husband's family — stopped her from making that decision. She couldn't abandon all of that. It was part of her children's heritage, what made them who they were, despite the sorrows. She couldn't let a gruesome ghost story from long ago ruin what they had today. Besides, the children loved it here, and so did she, despite the atmosphere with its occasional sinister overtones. And now that the Cunninghams had come to live at the cottage, there was company nearby. Only things were not turning out quite as she had planned. Charles and Sebastian were not getting on with Samuel as well as she had hoped. Perhaps she should have a word with Isabel about it, although that might only cause more awkwardness. In her experience children simply had to be left to get on with it, make their own decisions about friendships. You couldn't force it.

When Chris Morton had married her husband and come to live in this big looming house on Sheriffmuir, she had heard vague stories about a ghost known as the Weeping Woman and a curse she was supposed to have put on the family, but had given no thought to it. She didn't believe in ghosts, categorically did not. Old houses often carried stories with them, rumours of past tragedies,which left their mark on a place. So she had dismissed the story of Catherine Morton and thought nothing more about it ... until the day her husband died. Then the story came back to her with renewed force, and it no longer seemed so innocent but something which might just have had some impact on their lives ... It was one of the reasons why she had been so keen for the Cunninghams to take up residence in the cottage. She liked the idea of the company, not just for herself, but for her children too. Now, with the roads blocked and the moor covered in a blanket of immovable snow, she was more than ever glad of that extra company, particularly if the ghost of Catherine Morton was beginning to make her presence felt again.

A few days later the icy grip over Sheriffmuir began to weaken its hold and it looked like the promised thaw might arrive at last. Fiona and Samuel got their chance to return to Lynns Farm as planned.

Mr MacFarlane came out to meet them this time.

"Back again?" he commented gruffly, but they could tell from the look in his eye that he was not displeased to see them.

"Let me get something for you. Come along in now," and they followed him into the house.

They'd brought the pages of the journal to show him, and he took them gingerly in his hand, and laid them on the table. He read through them in silence.

"Well," he said. "This is quite a find."

The pages — crisp as a moth's wing and brindled with age — betrayed such a personal and intimate glimpse into Catherine Morton's domestic life that it made painful reading. "Any museum would be very interested in these, right enough. Could be quite valuable. I'm sure the archive in the Museum of Scotland would be glad of them to add to the information they already have."

"We wondered if you knew where she's buried?" Fiona said.

"It's her corpse you're after, now, is it? Poor woman."

"We just wondered, that's all ..."

"Can't leave it alone, can ye? Like terrier dogs with a bone, worrying away at it until you've got what ye'er after. Am I right?"

Fiona and Samuel lowered their eyes.

"You don't think she might be buried along with all the other Mortons, down in the family vault?" the old man countered.

"Something told us she might not be. I don't know why," Samuel muttered.

"You've a brain on ye, lad. You seem to be good at guessing your way around the place. Aye, perhaps it's a sixth sense ye've got there."

Mr MacFarlane sipped his tea and stared through the glass door of the stove. "Well, you're right as it happens. She and her baby were buried at Dunadd."

Samuel's eyes lit up but Mr MacFarlane held up a restraining hand. "Wait. They lie buried in an unmarked grave, according to my family anyway. Whether it's true or not, well ..."

"Then how will we ever find her?"

Mr MacFarlane shrugged. "It's not impossible. There should be some family records, I would have thought. Ironically enough, they are in fact the only Mortons to be buried at Dunadd. Maybe she liked it so much she just couldn't bear to leave it, hey?"

He paused for a moment. "She was one of those rare Mortons who knew Sheriffmuir well, and loved it for itself ... not because she owned it." He added, glancing at Fiona, "There are one or two Mortons born like that, now and again ... once in a while you come across one."

Fiona lowered her head shyly, accepting the compliment.

"I wish we knew where she was buried," Samuel went on. "We thought we could lay something on her grave, say some prayers, a little ceremony perhaps. We were hoping to do all this on the anniversary of their deaths — Catherine and her baby, I mean."

He looked at them. "13th January? That's tomorrow."

"We know."

"It's a nice thought but ..." He shook his head and sighed. "I wish I could help."

He seemed to hesitate and then said, "Come with me."

They followed him up the dark narrow stairs to a small landing. A big chest of drawers stood at the top in the shadows. He opened one of the drawers carefully.

"I'm reluctant to part with this. But if it'll help ..." He brought out a small silver dagger, with a twining serpent wrought around the handle and blade. "She gave it to him, as a gift." They looked at him in disbelief. "It's been in my family for generations."

Fiona took it, and studied the beautiful carvings on it.

"It's beautiful. We can't take this. It's too precious," Fiona said. "It must be worth a lot of money."

The old man shook his head slightly, and gave a knowing look. "There are some things more important than money. Aye, it's precious to my family, right enough, but let's just say this. If you find her grave, then bury this dagger along with her things that you found in the ebony box — that would mean a lot to my family, such as it is. If you don't find her grave, then you can return it to me, safe and sound."

A moment of understanding passed between the three, as the children realized how much trust he was placing in them.

"Thank you," was all they could say.

As they left, he stood at the door of his farmhouse, watching them go.

"Good luck," he called.

They waved and disappeared into the trees surrounding the farm, the precious dagger stowed away in Fiona's rucksack.

18. The Curse of the Mortons

Slowly they made their way back to Dunadd. They were tired and weary, thinking of all the sad things they had learnt.

As the pieces of the story slotted together like a jigsaw, a very black picture emerged. Dunadd had a past, a history, in which a young woman had suffered unspeakably at the hands of her own family.

"I wonder what Catherine and Patrick were like when they grew up?" Fiona said wistfully.

Samuel shrugged.

"They both died so young in the end," she mused sadly. "Nineteen years old, she must have been."

They walked on in silence for a while, retracing their steps to the waterfall. "It's funny. They're just dead people really. They lived so long ago, and yet I feel as if I know them. Their story seems so ... recent."

It was true. Because of the diary, they felt as if they knew her.

At the waterfall Fiona and Samuel looked around them sadly, remembering that this was the place where the couple had secretly met and married, where Patrick had placed the silver ring on her finger. This was where they had been discovered.

As soon as they arrived back at Dunadd Fiona and Samuel went straight to the library, but when they got there they found it was locked. Fiona rattled the door handle in frustration.

"She's started locking it again," she moaned.

"The key!" Samuel hissed. "Let's get it!" So they hurried down the stairs to the kitchen. There was no one about. Fiona whipped open the drawer of the dresser where her mother kept her bunch of keys, while Samuel stood guard at the door.

"Great!" Fiona cried, a look of despair on her face. The key to the library, the one key they were looking for, had been removed.

"What are we going to do now?"

It seemed that no matter how much Fiona and Samuel might want to resolve the mystery of the Weeping Woman and attempt to put her spirit to rest, everyone else was against them.

They needed to find some family records, anything that might point them in the direction of Catherine Morton's unmarked grave — but the one place where they might hope to come across any information of this sort was out of bounds. They were forbidden to go there, and without the library, they were lost. There was no way they could locate her grave by the following day.

Samuel hadn't given up hope yet.

"There must be a way round this," he reasoned. "Mr MacFarlane didn't give us the silver dagger for nothing. He's placing his trust in us."

"What's the use?" Fiona muttered. "It's like he said, the past just is; it can't be changed."

"So that's it then, is it?" he accused her. "We just give up?"

"Well, what else do you expect me to do?"

Samuel wandered off, frustrated by Fiona's willingness to abandon hope so easily. He knew it was difficult for her. This whole thing affected her family much more directly than it did him, but that was all the more reason for them to keep trying.

He found his mother in her work studio, surrounded by her own mess, fiddling with bits of wire.

"What's up?" she asked, as he strolled aimlessly between the workbenches, touching this and that.

He shrugged. "Nothing much!" *Just the end of the world,* he added inside his own head, but didn't bother to say it out loud. How could he confide in his mother all that he and Fiona had discovered over the past couple of weeks, since that night at Christmas when he had seen the Weeping Woman in the mirror over the fireplace. She would never believe him. It was all madness. Perhaps Fiona was right, and they should simply give up. What was it to him, anyway? He and his mother would probably move again in a couple of years' time, and he could forget all about Dunadd and its problems, leave it all behind.

He turned away, his head full of things he couldn't possibly say to his mother. She watched him for a while, shrugged, then bent to her work again.

A little later Samuel walked back across the courtyard, having made up his mind. He found Charles in the kitchen, making himself a sandwich.

"Is Fiona about?" he asked.

Charles looked at him darkly and shrugged. "How would I know?"

Samuel sighed and walked past him into the dark hallway beyond. Fiona was sitting on the stairs, her shoulders slouched against the banister.

"What's up?" he asked her, sitting down on the stair beside her.

She looked listless and fed up. "Nothing much!"

"Listen. I've been thinking," Samuel began.

"Oh yes?"

"What about if you asked your mum for help?"

"You are joking, aren't you?"

She lifted her head and stared at him. "She's locked me out of the library and hidden the key, forbidden me to visit Mr MacFarlane, and wears a face like thunder nowadays, and you think if I asked her, she might be prepared to help?"

She looked incredulous.

"Well, when you put it like that ... It's just she might know where any family records are kept. There's no harm in asking."

"Oh yes there is," Fiona murmured. "She'd eat me alive!"

Chris Morton was grooming one of the horses when Fiona crept up behind her in the fusty warmth of the stables. It was dark inside, only a triangle of light piercing the shadows from the open doorway.

"Mum ..." she began.

"Fiona, you startled me," she said, then carried on dragging the curry comb over Emperor's quivering flank.

"You should be doing this, you know," she said, half to herself.

"Sorry, I've just been a bit busy lately."

"With Samuel. Yes, I had noticed."

"There was something I wanted to ask you ..." she began, taking her life into her hands.

Her mother stopped grooming. "Is it about Mr MacFarlane?"

"Not ... *exactly* ..." But she didn't sound convincing.

"Then I don't want to hear it."

"Mum, please, there was something I wanted to ask you. We think there might be a way to resolve it all."

"*Resolve* it?"

"We want to put her to rest, Mum. But in order to do that we need to find her unmarked grave.

Mr MacFarlane thought there might be some family records ..."

Chris Morton shook her head and sighed at the mention of that man's name. "I'm never going to hear the last of this, am I?"

Fiona stood her ground.

"I'm sorry, Fiona. It's not on. I just want you to forget what Mr MacFarlane told you."

"But!"

"No buts, Fiona. Subject closed."

Fiona turned away and left the stables, hiding her look of devastation. She didn't want her mother to realize how much it meant to her.

Still nursing her disappointment, she knocked on the door of the cottage. Samuel opened it holding a piece of half-eaten toast in his hand.

He looked at her hopefully, but she shook her head.

"Any good?"

"Nope," Fiona said dismally. The two sat silently in his room, staring at the objects on his desk, the ring and the piece of tartan, the ebony box, the fragments of the journal and the silver dagger entrusted to them by Mr MacFarlane. It seemed as if they would never be able to use these things to help Catherine Morton. And if they couldn't use them, the curse would remain in place, hanging over Dunadd like a sword awaiting its time to fall.

Later that afternoon, as Granny Hughes was preparing vegetables for the evening meal, Fiona wandered into the kitchen looking gloomy.

"What's wrong with you?" Granny barked. "You've a face on you that would sour milk!"

Fiona didn't answer, but wandered through into the hallway. Her mother appeared from one of the side rooms.

"Fiona?"

She looked up.

"I've been thinking ... I still don't think it's a good idea, but ... there is something in the library, an amateur family history written by a man called Sir Douglas Morton, in 1889."

Fiona couldn't believe her ears.

She waited, holding her breath.

"It's never been published, but was written in longhand in manuscript form, and bound in vellum. It's a great thick tome, full of useless and boring information, like the names and dates of births and deaths, that kind of thing. You can look through it if you want. I've put it in the drawing room for you."

"Thanks, Mum," she cried.

"Handle it carefully. It's very old. And when you've finished with it, let me know. Don't try to replace it on the shelf or anything."

The room looked cold and cheerless. There was no fire lit, and the radiators creaked ineffectually. The boiler was too old and inefficient to heat the house properly. Fiona and Samuel approached the table where Chris Morton had left the big heavy-looking book for them. Now that they were able to finally inspect some genuine family records, they felt nervous, apprehensive about what they might find.

Fiona drew the book towards her, and carefully opened its crackling spine. The pages were very thick, yellowed with age, and brittle. She blew the dust from its cover.

They spread the volume on the floor between them, and leant forward. Mrs Morton had been right. A lot of it was very dreary, boring details of births and deaths, who had married whom, where and when. Eventually they found the name Catherine Morton, and read out what it had to say. *"Youngest daughter of Sir Charles and Lady Cecilia Morton. Born at Dunadd on the nineteenth day of April 1696. Died on the thirteenth day of January 1716."* There was no mention of her dying in childbirth, and no record of her stillborn son. There was also no acknowledgement of her secret marriage to Patrick. As far as her family were concerned, she had died a Morton, unwed.

They sat back on their heels and sighed. "This still doesn't tell us anything more about Catherine. And it certainly doesn't tell us where she might be buried."

"No, but read on ..." Samuel murmured.

They read a brief description of the death of Sir Charles Morton, who died only a couple of years after his daughter. He met his end in a riding accident. He rode his horse into the ravine near the waterfall one evening, which was considered strange as both horse and rider knew the moor well and were aware that the ravine was there. Mysteriously, the horse simply broke into a gallop and plunged them both to their deaths. It was never known why the pair had made such a fatal mistake.

As they read on, they learnt that Catherine's brothers had also died young. One in a hunting accident three years after he was married, leaving a widow and twin boys behind, the other drank himself to death. Samuel stared at what they had read and then looked at Fiona.

"D'you think we could be looking at the curse of the Mortons?"

Fiona had gone very pale. "This frightens me," she murmured.

Glancing through the family history, its thick pages crackling under their fingers, they saw that since

January 1716 there had been a string of untimely deaths among male members of the Morton family. Very few of them had lived to a ripe old age and died peacefully in their beds, although in many cases they did leave young children behind, otherwise the family name would not have survived. The records obviously only went as far as 1889, the year in which the manuscript was written, and Sir Douglas Morton the writer had been too dull to make the same connection as the children were now doing. He, after all, did not know the full story of Catherine Morton and her curse, but Fiona and Samuel did and their hearts stood still. Although the account stopped at the year 1889, and they had no way of knowing if history had continued to repeat itself in the years after this, there was also the evidence of the recent past — the death of Fiona's father.

Fiona looked towards the door of the room where her father died. He'd had a weak heart they said, but something had hastened him on his way.

"Are you thinking what I'm thinking?" Samuel said quietly.

Fiona's face was white. "Charles and Seb?" she whispered.

He nodded.

"It's as if they're doomed already."

"We have to find her grave before tomorrow," Samuel whispered.

"D'you think it'll do any good?" Fiona said doubtfully.

"It might."

They imagined the unhappy people who had lived in this house, and the ghost they had left behind. The ghost of one young woman, who couldn't rest in peace.

Samuel closed the book, disappointed.

"Well, we still don't know enough," he said. "We don't know where she's buried."

He reached up to replace the great leather book on the table. As he did so, he dropped it and it fell open on the floor with a heavy thud, its cover bent backwards.

"Careful!" Fiona hissed, grabbing at the volume.

Then she stopped, intrigued. A bundle of papers that had been pressed into the back of the book had slid out from between its pages and fluttered to the floor. She picked them up, Samuel watching her, and carefully, gently, so that they wouldn't break apart, she unfolded one or two of them.

"What are they?" Samuel asked.

"I don't know. Letters, I think."

The writing was very faded, and on closer examination they appeared to contain a lot of boring information about household expenses and domestic arrangements. What had seemed such an exciting find was nothing more than shopping lists, receipts, bills, lists of expenditure, that kind of thing. The signature at the bottom caught their attention — *Lady Cecilia.* It was she who had written these documents, plotting the finances of a busy thriving household. It would have been her duty to do so.

Samuel sighed. "It's amazing." He peered closer at the lists of figures, next to words like *flour* and *salt.* "Boring, though. Pity she couldn't have written down something more exciting to do with her daughter's death."

It *was* disappointing. Once they had noticed Lady Cecilia's signature they had both secretly hoped to discover some intimate account of how she had felt about the whole experience, her own thoughts and views on the subject of her daughter's "disobedience." But there was no such thing.

"Sir Douglas Morton must have come across these documents," Fiona mused "and thought they ought to be preserved, I suppose. More history about the house ..."

"Wait ..."

One of the documents stood out from the rest. Samuel laid it out flat and studied it for a moment.

"What is it?"

"A map."

"But what of?"

The markings were faded, but they could still make out the delicately-etched drawings of trees, a small cluster of buildings, and a familiar house with a tower. The whole thing had been hand-drawn on a piece of parchment and was an amateurish effort, but interesting nevertheless. At the top was a date, 1716.

"It's a map of Dunadd," Fiona said. "Look, there's your cottage."

They studied the map of Dunadd as it used to be in 1716, just after the time of the battle, noting the changes and the positioning of trees, boundaries and buildings. They saw a curving blue line to represent the Wharry Burn, and a watermill they hadn't known was there, a small settlement of cottages, a schoolhouse, a flour mill, a farm and a smithy. It was a thriving centre, a community so different from what they knew today. They stared, fascinated. In the top left-hand corner of the map, they saw a small cross, and beneath it the letter K.

"What does that mean?"

Fiona shrugged.

"Wait," Samuel said, and began flicking through the other documents. In the list of expenditures he came across the sentence "*thirteen ells of cloth for Kitty's raiment.*"

"Kitty? Who was Kitty?"

They stared at each other in silence, and realization dawned.

"We've found her," Samuel breathed. "We've found Catherine Morton."

19. An Unmarked Grave

From an upstairs window Charles watched his sister make her way beneath the bare trees with Samuel. He could see the tracks of their footprints in the snow, black marks that stood out clearly against the surrounding white.

He stood up swiftly, and hurried down the winding stone staircase of the tower.

Fiona and Samuel bore their latest treasure, the map of the unmarked grave, out into the garden. The silent shadows of the empty house seemed to wait for them to pass, as if they knew that something of significance was happening.

Outside, they unfolded the map, and looked carefully at the markings.

"It looks different," Fiona said. "There were more buildings then."

By the look of it Dunadd Estate used to be a busy and industrious place, with twenty or so workers living cheek by jowl in freezing-cold tiny cottages.

They stood at the back of the outbuildings, bearing the map between them, turning it this way and that, measuring distances. "You can see the foundation stones of these cottages in the grass behind your cottage," Fiona said. "When there's no snow, of course." The building had once been divided into three dwellings, where whole families were crowded into one room, with a few rolls of peat or a log fire to keep them from freezing in the long winter months.

"There was a watermill here," Samuel said, pointing at the map. "The burn was bigger then and used to run right through Dunadd. It must have powered the mill."

They followed the markings, trying to imagine how different life on the estate must have been then, three hundred years ago.

Above their heads came a dripping sound. The icicles that had hung on the trees for weeks were slowly beginning to melt.

"Looks like the big freeze might be over soon," Samuel murmured, a little wistfully.

According to the map Catherine was buried on the edge of Dunadd, on Glentye, the hill just above Dunadd.

They followed the map's pointers and strode under the beech trees along a bumpy track. It ended in a wide five-bar gate leading out onto open countryside.

They stood in the wind and listened to it sighing in the branches above them. They could see the Highland line from here, the range of snow-capped mountains, with the nearer peaks looming up large on the horizon.

One grey boulder stood at the spot, embedded in the ground, the only marker to show where Catherine's grave lay. No doubt her mother, Lady Cecilia would have wanted to lay flowers here. Would they have refused to talk about her, a forbidden subject too painful to mention? After all, she had been buried, with her baby, just beyond the gardens of Dunadd, like being placed permanently outside of Paradise.

"Tomorrow is 13th January," Fiona said softly. "The anniversary of their deaths. We can have our ceremony, after all."

They looked at one another, but even as she spoke she realized they were not alone. Charles had appeared behind them, as silently and stealthily as a fox in the shadows. He stood framed by the trees. They stared at him, and he stared back, his head full of the things he couldn't say.

"What's going on?" he whispered hoarsely, eyeing Samuel.

Fiona instinctively stepped between them. "He's only trying to help," she began.

"Help? How d'you make that one out?"

"Listen Charles. You have to listen. We've found out about the weeping woman."

"She's right, Charles," Samuel murmured. "Listen to her."

"This is where she's buried," Fiona cried, trying to get through to her brother. "Catherine Morton."

"I know," Charles said, his voice cold.

She stared at him. "What d'you mean, you know?"

"I know about the curse," he muttered. "I've read the journal. I've got a letter Dad wrote." From out of his pocket he produced a piece of paper that had been folded into quarters.

She looked shocked. "A letter?"

Charles nodded. "A letter he wrote the day he died."

"But how did you ...?"

"Same reason as you, I guess. I've been snooping around too." Then he eyed Samuel boldly. "We can all play at that game."

"What does it say?" Fiona breathed.

He passed it to her. "Read it for yourself."

As Fiona read the letter there was a silence between the three of them as they stood in the cold wind, their backs to it.

"I read the journal. I saw the things you took from the library. I followed you to Lynns Farm. I've been making my own search ..."

"Then you know the full story ...?"

"We're trying to put her to rest," Samuel murmured.

Charles laughed. "Put her to rest. And you really think that'll work?"

"Why not?" Fiona said. "It's better than doing nothing."

"We can't change anything," Charles said darkly, and it was only now that Fiona realized how much her brother had been suffering, how his eyes were ringed with shadows, from too many sleepless nights. "I have dreams," he murmured. "Like Dad did ... She says things. She stands at the foot of my bed, and speaks to me. You don't want to hear what she says," he adds, laughing in spite of himself.

Fiona and Samuel were silent. They didn't know what to say.

"She'll kill me one day," he breathed quietly. "And Seb too."

"Not if we make amends for the past," Fiona whispered.

But perhaps Mr MacFarlane was right. Maybe the sufferings of the past could never be resolved. "The past just is," he had said.

"We shouldn't have kept all this from you," she said softly, looking at her brother. "Perhaps we should have let you in on it at the beginning. We've been searching for clues to find out who she was, exactly, and why she was so sad."

"And did you?"

Fiona nodded. "She was in love with a farmer's son from Lynns Farm, the boy she mentions in the journal. Patrick MacFarlane. Her father and brothers refused to let her marry him, so she married him in secret. The family never acknowledged the marriage and locked her up in the house. He died fighting alongside the MacRae clan in the Battle of Sheriffmuir, while she watched the battle from an upstairs window. Two months later she died giving birth to a little boy who didn't survive. She died of grief."

Even Charles was shocked into silence by this bleak little account.

"I didn't know that," he murmured quietly. "I didn't know the rest of the story."

He looked down at the unmarked stone on the ground. The wind blew across the surface of the snow, stirring up powdery spirals, making a sad sound like a sigh.

20. Anniversary of the Dead

Samuel, Fiona, Charles and Sebastian gathered by the trees on the edge of Dunadd the next day. Despite the thaw the ground was still hard. They cleared away the snow and began to dig. They had one spade between them, and took turns in striking the earth.

When a big enough hole had been dug, they bowed their heads as the cold wind drove damp snow into their eyes. Fiona bent down and laid the carved ebony box in the ground. It contained the worn leather bag, the silver ring and the piece of tartan, as well as the slender bejewelled dagger, which Mr MacFarlane had given them. They had considered adding the pages of Catherine's journal to the treasures as well, but decided against it in the end. They didn't want her voice to be silenced for all time. The twelve-year-old Catherine had too much to say, and had never had the opportunity to say it.

Archaeologists and historians would have been glad of these artefacts, and would have happily displayed them in a museum, but the children knew they were precious for other reasons. When Patrick MacFarlane died in battle, they were all that Catherine had left of him — and she had cherished them. Although Patrick wasn't buried at this spot, the children felt that the dagger would represent him in some way, a symbol of his spirit, bringing the two together again.

Now the children laid these objects in the ground. They marked the spot with a small wooden cross on which they had written the words, "Here lie the remains of Catherine Morton and her son. Died 13th January 1716. Reunited in spirit at last with Patrick MacFarlane of Lynns Farm."

Fiona muttered a prayer, a psalm beginning "The Lord is my shepherd, I shall not want. He makes me lie down in green pastures ..."

It was trying to snow again, despite the thaw, and they shivered inside their coats. As the boughs of the trees bent in the wind, it was almost as if Sheriffmuir had remained unchanged, as if they were standing at Dunadd as it used to be three hundred years ago. As if the past three hundred years had never happened, and Catherine and her little baby had died only that morning.

Fiona placed a small twist of dried lavender beside the cross, left over from last year. There were no fresh flowers to be had on Sheriffmuir yet.

Then they shovelled earth back over the grave, burying the box and its hidden treasures. Charles hung his head, staring at the ground, his brow furrowed.

"D'you think it'll work?" Sebastian said. The Mortons looked at one another and Charles shrugged.

"I think so," Fiona murmured.

They stood for a moment or two in silence, then they turned and walked away, leaving the twist of dried lavender and the cross lying in the snow. A chill breeze still blew, and a disembodied voice seemed to whisper in the trees above, an answering prayer of gratitude ... but neither the Mortons nor Samuel heard it.

The day after they buried the ebony box, Samuel was finally able to go to school. An uneasy peace had been established at Dunadd, and Samuel regretted the fact that it was the end of the holiday. He was beginning to get used to it, being trapped on the moor. It had been a Christmas to remember!

"Well," his mother said as she drove him across the empty moor. Dirty piles of brown snow were heaped on either side of the road, where the snowplough had finally cut a path through. "You get to see your new school at last. I thought I was never going to get rid of you."

He gazed out of the window, his school bag at his feet, and said nothing.

"Back to reality," she said, grasping the steering wheel.

Samuel turned his head. Through the beech trees he caught a sudden glimpse of Dunadd, its white tower and turrets, the connecting stone archways, and the rooftop of their own little cottage. "I know one thing," he said suddenly, and his mother looked at him in surprise. "I'm glad we live on Sheriffmuir."

She raised her eyebrows, and turned to face the front. "I never thought I'd hear you say that."

Fiona was right when she expressed the hope that their little ceremony would work. They never saw or heard the Weeping Woman again. They believed they had buried her memory for good. Besides, she was no longer the Weeping Woman but had become Catherine Morton, who now lay buried with relics of her would-be husband, Patrick MacFarlane, and their son. The family who might have been but never were.

And Charles was no longer tormented by visions or dreams of her. His room at the top of the tower had become quiet ... for now.

As for the papers torn from Catherine's journal, these were given to a museum in Edinburgh, and are preserved behind glass. Catherine's diary entries are displayed, page by page, and kept in a controlled atmosphere so that they cannot deteriorate any further. Tourists stand and read what she has to say, and comment on what a bright and intelligent twelve-year-old she must have been.

Whenever Samuel and Fiona visited the exhibition, they felt proud of their own involvement in the discovery. If it hadn't been for them, another little piece of history would have been lost.

On one particular visit they peered through the glass at the familiar faded handwriting, gently spot-lit from above. The pages were pinned open like the wings of a butterfly, crisp with age. A white rectangle of card described what was on view.

A personal account of a twelve-year-old girl's life in the early eighteenth century. The pages on display are fragments of a journal written by Catherine Morton in 1708. They were found in the attic of Dunadd House on Sheriffmuir, near Stirling, and donated to the Museum earlier this year.

Behind them a middle-aged woman leaned forward.

"Read this, Geoffrey," she called to her husband. "What an intimate little account? It would make a *fabulous* story, wouldn't it?"

Samuel and Fiona exchanged glances.

"Mmm," Geoffrey murmured, pushing his bifocals up the bridge of his nose. He read in silence for a moment. "Spirited young woman. How old was she? Good Lord, only twelve years old."

"Come on," Fiona said quietly. "Time for a break."

As they wandered off to the coffee shop Samuel grinned with satisfaction.

"What's up with you?" she asked.

"I was just thinking — Catherine Morton has had her say at last. Her views are finally listened to."

Fiona was quiet. She was thinking about a passage she had just read that had given her pause for thought. *"They think I'm a witch because I hear voices sometimes. There are voices in the house, you see. I hear them, a boy and a girl, laughing, fighting, squeals of delight, sometimes quarrelling. Even banging. I am woken at night by their antics."*

Fiona stood still in the middle of the bright glass atrium. Samuel was rushing ahead of her and had chosen a table.

"Look," he called. "I've got the one with comfy sofas," and he threw himself into a squashy chair, looking gleeful. But Fiona was distracted. She hurried to catch up with him.

"Samuel?" she began ...

Author's Note

I would like to acknowledge certain invaluable sources of information, used when researching this book. The information on page 97 was based on *The Jacobites,* Anthony Kamm, National Museums Scotland Publishing, 1995, (p.15), and the quotation on page 97 was taken from *The Street and Place Names of Dunblane and District,* Archie McKerracher, Stirling District Council, 1992, (p.43). The information on page 96 was also based on *The Street and Place Names of Dunblane and District.*

I would like to thank my editor, Gale Winskill, and of course friends and family for their support and encouragement, in particular my children Micah and Martha.

MISSING

HAVE YOU SEEN THIS CAT?

IF SO PLEASE CALL 0131 234 5677

£30 REWARD

Catscape

Mike Nicholson

Fergus can't believe it when his brand-new digital watch starts going backwards. Then he crashes (literally) into gadget-loving Murdo, and a second mystery comes to light — cats are going missing all over the neighbourhood. As the two boys start to investigate, they find help in some unexpected places.

Mike Nicholson won the Kelpies Prize with Catscape, his first novel, which is set in his home neighbourhood of Comely Bank, Edinburgh.

Contemporary Kelpies

Winterbringers

GILL ARBUTHNOTT

St Andrews, Fife — not known for its glorious weather, but even so, Josh hadn't expected the sea to start to freeze and ice to creep up the beaches ... His summer holiday isn't looking too promising, especially as his only companions are a strange local girl, Callie, and her enormous dog, Luath.

Then they uncover the journal of an eighteenth-century girl who writes about a Kingdom of Summer, and suddenly find themselves thrown headlong into a storm of witches, ice creatures, magic and the Winter King. A permanent winter threatens unless they can help restore the natural balance of the seasons.

Can they stop the Winterbringers once and for all?

"An unusual, enjoyable combination of fantasy thriller and psychological drama with a warmly satisfying ending." — *The Scotsman*

"Dramatic, well crafted, well sustained and imaginative. Her relationships are utterly convincing, written without affectation or self-consciousness." — *Times Education Supplement Scotland*

Contemporary Kelpies

Dragonfire
Anne Forbes

"Well, I didn't ask to be a pigeon! ... I wanted to be an eagle, didn't I? ... Why couldn't we have been eagles instead of pigeons? What a life! Nothing but cooo, cooo and peck, peck, all the time. ..."

"... This is the High Street not the Highlands! We're not here to cause a sensation, and ... if it weren't for your stupidity, we wouldn't be here in the first place!"

Stroppy pigeons in Edinburgh's Old Town. It's not a normal part of daily life — but things are never going to be the same again.

Clara and Neil have always known the MacArthurs, the little people who live under Arthur's Seat, in Holyrood Park, but they are not quite prepared for what else is living under the hill. Feuding faery lords, missing whisky, magic carpets, firestones and ancient spells . . . where will it end? And how did it all start?

Set against the backdrop of the Edinburgh Fringe and Military Tattoo this is a fast-paced comic adventure, full of magic, mayhem and mystery — and a dragon.

Contemporary Kelpies